Blood of My Shadow

The Rise & Fall of the Syndicate

Book I

Jovon Scott

Edited by Larry L. Franklin

Urban Street Lit
An imprint of History Publishing Company LLC

ISBN: E-Book 9781940773896
ISBN: Paperback 9781940773889

History Publishing Company LLC
PO Box 700
Palisades, NY 10964

Ordering Information:
Quantity sales. Special discounts are available on quantity purchases by corporations, associations, and others. For details, contact the publisher at the address above.

Orders by U.S. trade bookstores and wholesalers. Please contact Big Distribution:
Tel: (845) 359-1765; or visit historypublish@aol.com.

About the Author

"Writing is the avenue that changed my life, and I don't plan on slowing down anytime soon." Jovon Scott

***

Jovon Scott is 30 years of age and began his incarceration in an Illinois prison at age 18. He has a projected parole date of 2033. Jovon was raised on the slum streets of Chicago in an area better known as the Robert Taylor Projects where unemployment reached 95%, an African-American population of 96%, 40% single-parent families, and a public assistant family income of $5,000 per year. It comes as no surprise that Jovon turned to street gangs that offered a means of survival, a family-like environment, money, drugs, sex, and respect.

Jovon gives credit to the gang culture for forcing him to want more out of life, and a willingness to pursue it with gusto. Discipline was front and center in the street gangs of the 1980s and 90s. Being self-educated, Jovon continues to prepare himself for a more favorable future upon his release.

It was in a 6 x 9 foot double-occupancy cell where Jovon discovered how writing frees the soul and opens an imaginary reality, a breeding place for creativity. "*Blood of my Shadow: The Rise & Fall of the Syndicate*" is a work of urban fiction, focusing on the underbelly of the urban culture. It is here where Jovon combines lessons learned on the streets of Chicago, an unharnessed imagination, and his ability to spin an exciting story.

Acknowledgements

I wish to thank the History Publishing Company for publishing my book and providing a lifeline from the street culture that has plagued me since adolescence. I acknowledge my editor, Larry L. Franklin, for his support and guidance throughout the completion of my work. You will forever be part of my writing journey. Many thanks to Chicago model, Tianna Cooks, for allowing her photo to be on the book cover.

Thanks goes to Celeste Radcliffe for her undeterred support and the constant fixture you have been in my life. You have been the mother for me when I never had one. I love you. Words cannot express my deep feelings for Tianna V. Cooks. Ever since childhood, our energies have always brought us together on the same plain field of existence. You inspire me and make me a better man. Thanks for believing in me and being a positive force in my life. I love you.

For Aunt Ruth and Lizzy, may her soul rest in peace, you have always been family to me when I was forsaken by others. My imperfections as a child were never a permanent stain on your hearts. Thank you both. I love you. Natasha Fertil held me down and kept me mentally grounded when I needed it the most. Hopefully you are happy and life is treating you well. You will forever be a special person to me.

Thanks to Emmie Lipscolm and Shamel for holding me down when things were bad and I didn't have anyone to turn to. I will forever be grateful. And to my brother Brandon Johnson and my second mother, Angelique Johnson, I thank you for the past memories that I hold on to each day. I look forward to building a stronger bond with both of you. Love you.

Thanks to Shanquia Franklin and Tykisha Kemp who held me down for a number of years. It was an amazing feeling to have been accepted by your family. To Jessica Wilson, Whittney Howard, Sharmetta, Ms. Rhonda Wilson – my right hand and closest – Sharita Lofton, Jasmine Jackson, Katie Marshall, Dominique Binns, Octavia and Angela Williams, Gwendolyn Richardson and Latoya Weaver, I thank you all for the letters, pictures and over all support.

To my brothers – Lorenzo Guye, Kenyatta Brown, Prince Johnson, Westside, Terry Brooks, Murda Maxx, Polo, Boon, Cino, Varro, 400, Sincere, Jumar House, Tom Slick, Psycho, James Campbell, Ontario Walls, L.C., JoJo, Quack, Jamil Fleming, T-Killa, Justin Jackson, Diddy, Spookie, Lil Johnny, Webb, Mook-Marvin Stone, Rosco, Randy Rice, Bosco, and lastly, Leo, Lb, Big Tree, Bay Bay and Brandon Lewis. If I missed you in this one, I got you in the next.

Jasmine, Tanisha, Janece, Torri, Special, Shamirah and Faith. I love you all with all that's humanly possible. To my nieces and nephews, this is for y'all as well. Georgette Hill you will always be number one lady and as my mother that will never change.

I'm here to stay in this writing game. Buff City, Freedom Town and O.T.F. we the family…

Contents

Prologue

War is a cause and blood is the ink used to write the markings on the wall. Blood spills on both sides – those who are innocent and our enemies as well. There will be casualties determined by providence, leaving us unable to choose who stays and who goes. We live by a set of rules and principles that not only govern our longevity in the underworld, but shapes who we are as a player in the game of chances. Death is synonymous with the culture we live in; blood is only repaid in blood.

We are Penumbras, mere fractions of a shadow. But when united, we become one full and complete shadow, absorbing the magical and spiritual strength emulated by a total eclipse. And when Penumbras die, they become the ***Blood of my Shadow.***

Mona Moore, Sole Proprietor of The Sheridan Syndicate.

***

The Sheridan Syndicate engaged in illegal activities for profit. While sometimes referred to as the mafia, mob, gang, or the underworld, The Syndicate had no equal. Under Mona Moore's leadership, the organization accumulated some $100 billion in capital; provided the umbrella under which criminal activities operate; all for the sole purpose of granting the means to an end – control and power. The Meddstone Drilling Company and the Royal Diamond Casino & Resort were legitimate business organizations that provided cash flow and an avenue for money laundering. They too fell within the scope of the Syndicate.

The extravagant lifestyle and accumulation of wealth were mere by-products. Underground drug traffic, money laundering, robbery, murder, blackmail, political misdeeds, investments, and inflows from outside investors led to the ultimate goal – control and power, an addiction that Mona Moore wholeheartedly admits.

While Mona maintained tight control of the Syndicate's operations, her twin sons, Ty and Sky, assisted her. The enforcers, Kema and Anisa, protected the family and added to the core of professionals who ran the organization. Business associates, criminals, soldiers, policeman, politicians, investors, and other centers of influence made the system work.

In addition to the federal government, the Cuadras and Mendoza Cartels were the Syndicate's largest competitors. It was their job to destroy, lock up, or kill members of The Sheridan Syndicate. The Carlos Cuadras family, the Mendoza brothers and a large supporting cast controlled the Cartels. Drug traffic had broadened domestic terrorist activities, reaching into the international communities. Blood spilled could fill a river running from the east to the west coast, spilling over into the Gulf of Mexico and the Pacific Ocean.

This is a fictional story about control and power, accompanied by sex and violence, a lustful lifestyle, the willingness to die for your cause, and the hope of a lasting legacy.

The Sheridan Syndicate

Five months earlier…
Juneau, Canada
January 1, 2012
10:45 am

In a world built on imperialism and capitalism, opportunity was there for the taking. Grasp the thing you desire, hold onto it. Mona Moore, the sole proprietor of The Sheridan Syndicate, was an optimistic opportunist in the endeavors that most people considered unachievable. She launched one of the most lucrative empires of her era; wealth and connections in the political and corporate worlds; and control of an underground drug trade.

Mona stood five foot, eight inches with a well-toned body. Her honey-brown eyes and full lips complemented her elegant taste in attire and youthful appearance. At 45, she looked to be in her mid 20s. Mona's two sons, Ty and Sky, handled the more respectable and legal ventures – Meddstone Drilling Company and the Royal Diamond Casino and Resort. The combined net worth of the brothers' companies was between one and two billion dollars.

The Sheridan Syndicate had an on-going feud with The Cuadras Cartel and The Mendoza Cartel, both based out of Mexico and led by Carlos Cuadras.

The helicopter landed on the roof of the massive estate located in Juneau, Canada just off the Gulf of Alaska. Mona entered the main conference room and took her seat at the head of the table. The Syndicate members stopped talking.

"Ladies and Gentlemen," Mona said, "let's begin the meeting."

"We had a problem docking one of the shipments last week," Sigmund Stein said. Sigmund was head of the Stein family that controlled the drug trade in New York and Maine. "The Coast Guard stopped the ship and discovered the containers that held the product."

"What's the loss?" Mona inquired with a calm and steady voice.

"Approximately $7.8 million," Ty interjected. "I was responsible for seeing to it that things with the Coast Guard were taken care of, which had been done." Ty's anger grew. "The problem is this. Mr. Stein was given a specific set of instructions that he failed to follow."

"That's bullshit," Stein interrupted. "My people followed every instruction given to them. It's not a problem from my end."

"We're not going to start a shouting match," Mona said. "We suffered a loss and there's nothing we can do to get it back." Anisa, one of Mona's enforcers, took her phone and left the room. Mona turned her attention to Vino, head of the Arturo family that ran the drug trade in Nevada, Utah, and Colorado. "How are the permits and renovations coming along with the casino and resort?" Mona asked, as she appeared ready to move on.

"I'm suppose to meet with Governor Perez and the Gambling Commissioner soon," Vino answered. "Things are on schedule."

Anisa returned to the conference room, pulled a gun from her shoulder holster and blew Mr. Stein's brains across the table. She then put her weapon away and pressed the intercom button. "I need a clean up team in the main conference room," Anisa insisted. A group of maids and butlers hurried into the room, scrubbing and dragging Stein's body away. As the cleanup continued, Anisa addressed the group. "My contacts advised me that the containers had been tipped off by an anonymous caller. The call was traced back to a burner phone. The cell towers indicated that the call came from Mr. Stein's warehouse, where the containers were found as well."

"Well, he got what he deserved," Mona said in her business-like manner. "What's the status on the situation concerning the drilling? Why haven't the trucks been called in to drill?" she asked.

"There's a property line issue," Sky answered. "We hope to resolve it soon."

"The Cuadras and Mendoza Cartel's?" Mona asked.

"Currently, the only feuds are in Texas, the other states and cities are quiet," Kema explained. Kema, the younger sister of Anisa, was Mona's enforcer as well.

"How close are things to the drilling sites?" Mona asked.

"They're close," Kema confirmed.

"Make sure this doesn't hinder the drilling," Mona said as she stood to leave. With that, the meeting concluded.

***

Chicago, Illinois
January 3, 2012
3:00 pm

There was nothing that held any sense of familiarity. The people he once knew, the polluted air he once inhaled, even the place he called home seemed foreign, lost, drifting into the unknown. His name was Kenyatta Brown, better known as Yatta, a free man, having served a 20-year sentence for a murder he did not commit. A controlled rage shadowed him while his anger grew like wild grass. So many people had crossed him. But now, at age 39, Yatta had no margin for error and no room for another bid. His priorities were focused on the most essential thing – survival.

Through numerous letters and prison visits, Key had become Yatta's friend/student. His mentorship and guidance made Key into who she had become. At 37, she demanded respect and held little tolerance for weakness. She was vibrant and ready to live. Now that Yatta was a free man, their friendship was without boundaries.

Key's strong physical appearance and dominant ways led some to believe her to be a lesbian. Her swagger, aggressive demeanor and choice of attire added to her persona. But Yatta never questioned her sexual preference, believing that it was not a line he should cross. Key stood five feet, nine inches, a yellow-brown complexion, hazel eyes, and long, jet-black hair braided underneath a baseball cap. Once you looked past Key's perceived toughness, her beauty was obvious.

When a man festers in his anger, he grows confident in his hatred. He boils in anticipation to act on the thoughts he plays over and over in his head – then they're manifested…

"The Sheridan Syndicate Meets The Cuadras & Mendoza Cartels."

Miami, Florida
January 4, 2012
1:30 pm

Although Ty and Sky were identical twins, they carried contrasting personas. Ty was more reserved. Sky, on the other hand, was more out spoken, unpredictable, and the more aggressive of the two. Both brothers were over six feet tall with board shoulders and a muscular build. Vinny Cuadras, son of Carlos and a member of The Cuadras Cartel had contacted them. Ty and Sky knew Mona wouldn't approve of this meeting, and that Vinny didn't have the balls to ask Mona for a sit down.

Kema and a few of her men escorted the brothers. (Kema, sister of Anisa, was an enforcer for The Sheridan Syndicate, of Russian decent and loyal to Mona.) Although she was only 26-years old, her experience in warfare was unmatched. Her long, jet-black hair, green eyes, and physical appearance were that of a cross-fit marathoner. Kema was a beautiful woman.

After checking their weapons, Kema and her men were ready to go. "Where is Sky?" Kema asked.

"He should be here any minute," Ty answered. Sky was never one to show up on time. Sure enough, a white Bentley Azzure sped around the corner and stopped next to Kema and Ty. "Good of you to join us," Ty taunted.

"I got a life too," Sky replied.

The brothers and their men jumped into the black SUV and headed to the meeting. Ty took a deep breath, anticipating tension. They pulled in front of Vinny's five-star diner and made their entrance. Once inside, the brothers were escorted to a private room where Vinny waited.

"Nice of you to join us," Vinny said. "Sorry about the company, but I see you brought guests as well." Vinny was very vindictive and mendacious; nothing Ty didn't know.

"Let's get to the point as to why we're here," Ty said as he pulled at his suit jacket.

"No small talk?" Vinny asked. "But you're so serious Kema. Smile a bit. You're a beautiful woman; don't look so ugly. The reason I contacted you guys and not Mona, is because she can be…."

"Let me stop you right there," Sky said as he cut Vinny off. "You keep her name out of your mouth."

"You're the owners of the largest import and export docks along the Pacific and Atlantic Coasts," Vinny said. "We're looking to buy into one of the properties. You set the price and we'll pay it. Also, we'll establish long-term peace treaties from coast to coast."

Ty chuckled in disbelief. "You're joking, right? Because if you aren't, then you've wasted our time."

"Gentlemen," Vinny said. "Let's be reasonable. Trade and commerce establish all great nations. We have our differences. I get it. But this is business, nothing to take personal."

"Regardless of history and the nations you're referring to," Ty said, "we're not in the business of brokering commercial properties."

"Let's not fight amongst ourselves. Let's reason and compromise with each other for the greater good. We both have shed too much blood," Vinny added.

"Wars result in casualties and bloodshed," Ty said. "We can't negotiate in terms of conflict."

Vinny grew quiet. His mood changed as he pointed his finger in Ty's face. "You listen to me you piece of shit. Either you agree to sell one of them docks or we'll operate over your heads and burn down every piece of property you own from coast to coast."

Without hesitation, Ty removed his butterfly knife and plunged it into Vinny's hand. Vinny screamed in agony as Ty now had his Ruger pressed to the back of Vinny's head. The room was in complete pandemonium. Vinny's men took aim as Kema and Sky followed in unison. "Here's what's about to happen," Ty explained. "You're going to tell your men to put their guns down and kick them across the room."

"Put your guns down," Vinny ordered.

Ty pulled his knife from Vinny's hand and wiped the blood on Vinny's shoulder. "This meeting never happened. Consider that something to be thankful for," Ty said as he and his men made their exit.

In war, you never forget the price it cost to battle, or the value you pay to win. But no matter the balance, you must maintain power, control, and respect in order to defeat disdain. Malice is but a tool forged to cultivate the ultimate height of war…

***

Chicago, Illinois
January 9, 2012
12:43 a.m.

Yatta drove through the streets of Chicago. While his mind dwelled in the past, thoughts were fixated on his current freedom. He had been awarded a second chance. Still, a few chapters in his life needed to be closed.

"So, what's our move now that you're home?" Key inquired.

"I figured I would just allow things to unfold and go from there."

"I can't believe you're home," Key raised her voice in excitement.

Nobody knew that Yatta's appeal for a new trial had been granted. His appellate attorney found some constitutional deficiencies throughout his original trial, making Yatta a free man.

"What about Chuck and Nate?" Key asked. Yatta was silent. Words could not explain how he felt about their betrayal. Chuck and Nate crossed him without regrets. Yatta's silence was all too familiar; something that Key knew all too well. "Understood," Key said as if Yatta had given her a specific set of instructions.

If I have repaid my friend with evil or plundered my enemy without cause, let my enemy pursue my soul and over take it, and let him trample my life to the ground and lay my glory in the dust...

***

Havana, Cuba
January 10, 2012
2:15 pm

The Cuadras Cartel operated in conjunction with The Mendoza Cartel, two of Mexico's most feared organizations. Carlos' father was Italian and his mother was Mexican, providing his connection to the streets of Mexico, and the Italians who dwelled in the underworld. Carlos started his empire as a teenager, and wasted no time growing the Cuadras to what it is today. While Carlos had faith in his son, Vinny needed to be more disciplined and reserved; not quick to make irrational decisions.

Carlos and Mona were active in both the political and criminal realms. While they were friends and business partners eons ago, their relationship had moved from strained to arch nemesis. Carlos' goal was to seize control of the black markets in the United States, retire and turn the family business over to Vinny. Although Carlos was 53 and wealthy beyond imagination, he remained addicted to the power and control that the criminal activities afforded him.

Carlos and Vinny flew to Havana, Cuba to discuss business with a few investors interested in using a money laundering service Carlos offered. Once the meeting was over, Carlos spoke to Vinny about a move he made against Mona. "Why do you insist on provoking Mona?"

Vinny knew what he was taking about, not to mention the fact that his hand was wrapped in bandages and his father had never inquired about it. "I only asked for the meeting with her sons, thinking that I could get them to budge," Vinny said. "Besides, they are the owners. And we need access to one of those docks. I was acting in support of the family."

"Stupidity is one thing, but life altering acts are another," Carlos said. "The reason I'm so hard on your decision making is because as a leader, you must evaluate your every move. You have to articulate yourself with precision. The art of thinking wins wars. Brute force never over powers finesse."

"So what should I do now?" Vinny asked.

"In this world, blood is only repaid in blood," Carlos replied.

"So I should retaliate?"

"That is up to you," Carlos said. "So, how is business?" Carlos asked, switching the subject.

"Business is good as usual."

"Good," Carlos said. "I have to get going. Keep in mind the conversation we had. There's more to life than having to exist in someone else's shadow. Create your own legacy and let go of the things that don't define you." Carlos left Vinny to contemplate his prior actions.

A man who teaches a son nothing, endorses him to fail, and a son who fails the teachings of his father, never had any respect for the man that taught them…

"Rage Has No Boundaries."

Riverdale, Illinois
January 12, 2012
11:45 pm

"Baby, where you at?" Chuck yelled out to his pregnant wife, Lynda. He just closed the deal on a house where they would spend the rest of their lives.

"I'm in the kitchen. Stop yelling before you wake the kids," Lynda said as she walked into the living room.

"I talked with our realtor. I closed the deal on the house," Chuck said with an air of excitement.

"That's great, but what about this property and the other things we have going on?"

"Let your man handle that. You just focus on getting ready to move to California," Chuck said as he lifted the lid to the pot on the stove.

"Your plate is in the oven," she said as the phone began to ring.

"Wad up?" Chuck asked.

"We had a problem at the spot," Chris said. Chris worked for Chuck and ran the spots. "We got hit and one of our workers got killed."

"Get over here – now!" Chuck said as he slammed the phone down. "Chris is stopping by for a minute." Lynda looked concerned. Chuck never brought outside work to his home – ever.

"Is everything alright?"

"Yeah, yeah. I just need to have a sit down with Chris. Besides, he's about to be running things now that I will be out of the picture." She knew of his illicit activities on the streets, the dirt that filled his past, but she learned to accept it. He touched her growing belly and looked into her eyes. "Baby, I promise. I'm done with this life. I'm going to live right by you and the kids. I'm tired of the streets. It's all about us now." His eyes filled with tears as he kissed her stomach.

The doorbell rang. He peered through the peephole. "It's Chris." As Chuck opened the door, a masked assailant pushed Chris' lifeless body into the foyer. The assailant then pointed the weapon at Chuck. The silencer smoked with anticipation of completing another promise.

"If you're here for me," Chuck said, "then you know I got money and I'm done with this shit. My family and me are moving away. You can have all I got." As he was about to speak, Lynda screamed. She saw Chris' dead body on the foyer floor. As the assailant pointed the gun, ready to squeeze the trigger, Chuck jumped in front of Lynda. "Come on man, she's pregnant. Look, I got one-hundred-and-fifty grand in a safe downstairs. It's all yours. Don't nobody else need to get hurt." The assailant followed Chuck and Lynda to the downstairs safe. Chuck opened the safe and stepped back. "It's all there. We should be square." Chuck reached out to his wife, hoping to get out alive.

The assailant removed the mask and threw it to the floor. Chuck saw a familiar face and immediately knew that death was close. It was Key, Yatta's friend and Chuck's enemy. Key's visit wasn't about money; it was retribution for crimes against Yatta. She came to collect a debt owed in blood. Everything else was collateral damage.

Chuck turned to Lynda. "I'm sorry you got caught up in this mess." As he fell to his knees, Lynda leaned over, lifted his chin, and starred into his eyes. Lynda was no longer afraid; a newfound strength brought her peace.

"I forgive you," Lynda said, wanting Chuck to hear her before it was too late. She moved forward and kissed his lips. Their embrace was cut short by heat and hot metal. Key made certain they were dead. She then climbed the stairs knowing that her job was unfinished. All loose ends must be tied; mistakes could be hazardous. Key found the kids' room and sent them to be with their parents.

***

Chicago, Illinois
January 13, 2012
1:37 pm

When you define *loyalty*, what do you mean; faithful to a friend, a cause? *Loyalty* can't be defined or acted upon as a courageous act. Most people relying on *loyalty* die or place themselves in a circumstance worst than death.

Key pulled up on her motorcycle and found Yatta sitting on the hood of his Benz. She removed her helmet and walked towards him carrying a backpack. "That's a hundred- and-fifty grand," Key said as she dropped it at his feet. She then gave him a newspaper, pointing out an article for Yatta to read.

> *On the 1900 block of Edbrooke In Riverdale, Illinois a couple, along with their children and friend were found gunned down in their home. The victim's were identified as 40-year old Charles Davis Jr. and his wife Lynda, their 10 year old son Jason Davis, and thirty seven, year old Christopher Green. The authorities say it appears to have been a robbery gone badly. At this moment, they have no leads.*

Yatta read the article, pulled out his lighter and set the newspaper on fire. Key knew to never speak of this again, and she didn't.

"So, what's next?" Key asked.

"How long it's been since you saw Capone and Deno?" Yatta said. Capone and Deno were brothers and ran with Yatta before he was sent away. Yatta had taken a liking to the duo. They had started running things for him while he was incarcerated. Yatta never questioned their absence during his prison bid. He knew street niggaz didn't like anything about prison, not even dealing with the niggaz they had inside.

"I see them from time to time, but we haven't hung out for years," Key admitted. Yatta gave her the backpack filled with money and tossed her his car keys.

"Let's take a ride," Yatta said as they got into the car.

A Drug Deal Gone Bad

Miami, Florida
February 1, 2012
2:36 pm

Mona's estate was impressive. Massive iron gates surrounded the perimeter and large lion statutes discouraged unwelcome guests; manicured lawns hugged a circular driveway constructed of cobblestone and heated tiles; and two large oak and granite doors guarded the home's entrance. The architecture and furnishings were striking.

Sky walked into the mansion and saw Kema. They had not seen each other since the meeting with Vinny.

"You're here to tell Mona about the meeting, aren't you?" Kema inquired with a concerning tone.

"I have to tell her. If she hears about it on the streets, she'll flip out," Sky replied. Kema knew he was right. As Sky walked into Mona's office, she was studying a large map. Sky took a deep breath. "What are you up to?" Sky asked.

"Plans for the future, " Mona responded, looking towards her son. "Why are you really here?" she asked. Mona always knew when something was wearing heavy on her son.

Sky looked at the floor for a moment before he spoke. "We had a meeting with Vinny not too long ago. He wanted one of the docks, and things got out of hand. Ty stabbed him in the hand. Guns were drawn. But we handled it."

Mona listened as Sky explained things. When he finished, Mona failed to reply, leaving Sky to wonder what she was thinking. She then pressed the intercom button, calling Kema who entered the office with a look of self-condemnation plastered across her face. "Killing the both of you right now would be too easy," Mona said. "And I'm not in the mood to clean the mess up. So, I'm just going to remain calm and deal with this accordingly. From this day forward, nobody is to meet with members of The Cuadras Cartel without my approval – and I mean nobody. I'm on the brink of something that would solidify our future. So, I don't need any unnecessary distractions. Now you two can leave my office before I change my mind about killing you."

Sky and Kema hurried from the room. "That went well," Sky said.

"You're a rat!" Kema said as she pushed him.

"At least this rat kept us alive." Sky yelled as they left the mansion.

Mona picked up the phone and called Anisa. "I need you to pay our friend Vinny a visit." Mona hung up the phone.

Be careful when you seek attention, because you just might get it…

***

Chicago, Illinois
February 3, 2012
9:47 pm

The night air was heavy. A mixture of urine and polluted waste created an unbearable stench. Footsteps splashed through puddles of water mixed with human piss. Time stood still, as if life had been placed on hold. Alleys can be a world within a world, occupied by people who cherish cardboard boxes they call home and patrons who use the back door to Club Radius.

Club Radius was an elite gentleman's club owned by Vinny, but managed by a man called Q. The Club was a front where Vinny laundered money and pushed his product in the Midwest region.

Two Range Rovers pulled into the alley and parked near the back entrance of the club. Q got out of his truck and turned his nose up at the two men sleeping in a box near the dumpster.

"Johnny, what's good dawg?" Q asked.

"Nothing much. Getting to the money. That's about it," Johnny replied. He then popped the back latch to the truck and grabbed two duffel bags. "That's three-hundred grand!" Johnny noted as he put the bags into Q's truck. "I'll get you your product in a couple days. I'm waiting on Vinny," Q explained.

"That sounds goo..." Johnny's words were cut short as a bullet ripped through his neck. Johnny grabbed his neck and began coughing up blood. Moments later he fell to the ground – dead.

While Q ran to his truck and tried to open the driver's door, one of the bums hidden in the cardboard box opened fire. The other shooter took aim with an assault rifle and hit Q twice. Q rolled over and saw Capone, one of the men posing as a bum.

"I know you man. I know you!" Q repeated.

"What good does that do you?" Capone said as he shot Q in the head. Meanwhile, his accomplice, Brandon was taking the duffel bags from the truck. Once everything was loaded into the car they had parked behind the building, they pulled off in a hurry.

They had been watching Q and Johnny for weeks. Now all of their hard work had paid off. Brandon shuffled through the bag. He was ecstatic. "Yo, we rich my nigga," Brandon said. "I'm about to ball out of control dawg. This got to be about half a million."

Capone pulled behind an old building and parked. "Open the glove compartment and grab them wipes so we can clean the car of our prints," Capone said.

Brandon opened the glove compartment. Capone pulled out his Ruger.

Boom!

Boom!

Brandon's brains were blown all over the front windshield. A car driven by Capone's brother, Deno, was parked behind them. Capone signaled the car and the lights came on as Deno pulled up. "Grab the bags, I got to clean the car," Capone said.

A rich man wouldn't consider taking any risk to lose his fortune, but a broke man, he'll take all the risk in the world…

***

West Virginia
February 4, 2012
10:00 am

Mona was funding Paul Kowski's bid for the Governor of West Virginia. While Kowski was leading in the polls, he was disliked among the general population. He was known to be a gambler and womanizer.

Kowski pulled in front of his campaign headquarters. Since he had given the campaign organizers the day off, the building was empty. When Kowski entered his office he was surprised to see Mona and Kema.

"You've been avoiding my calls Mr. Kowski," Mona said as she sat at his desk.

"I've been kind of busy," he replied nervously.

"Have a seat, don't be so rude," Mona said. "Kema this is Paul Kowski. Paul this is Kema."

Kowski was uncomfortable for all the right reasons. "Mona, I've had some time to think. I can't be tied to you. It'll end my political career and all of the things I've worked so hard for. I'm willing to pay back your contributions."

"That's understandable," Mona said as she stood to leave. She stopped and whispered something into Kema's ear and left the room. Kema looked at Kowski and smiled.

"Is she mad at me?" He suspected.

"No. We take nothing personal – all business." Kema then pulled the gun from the small of her back and shot Kowski dead.

Pandemonium At The Fiesta

Chicago, Illinois
February 7, 2012
6:47 pm

Capone and Deno were closer than brothers. They were best friends. Capone was 37 with dark skin and rough features. His long braids and dark eyes told a gruesome story of things gone wrong. Deno, at age 35, had a dark complexion as well; stood some six feet tall, muscular built, and a low hair cut. Deno wasn't much of a talker. But whatever he said was worth hearing.

When the brothers arrived at their apartment, they found the front door open. Both Capone and Deno pulled their guns out. Capone's heart was pounding with anticipation. The brothers had robbed so many people and brought them harm; no telling when retaliation would come knocking at their door.

As they walk it into their kitchen, Key turns the lights on. "Y'all look nervous," she said.

"Better nervous than dead. You sure know how to make an entrance," Capone said as he tucked his gun and hugged his childhood friend.

"This got to be important if you're here," Deno chimed in.

"See for yourself," Key said. She led them into the living room where the brothers saw Yatta. Capone was flooded with emotions, falling to his knees. Deno was shocked and walked up to his surrogate brother and hugged him. Yatta pulled Capone to his feet.

"We don't belong on our knees, ever! A man stands on his feet no matter the circumstances," Yatta said to Capone, hugging him tightly.

"What's the plan?" Deno asked. He knew Yatta was ready to get the ball rolling and establish their standings in the world.

"We played by all the rules and still lose. I'm ready to live," Capone explained.

"That's what we're going to do," Yatta said. "Starting with Peter Rosenthal."

"Peter Rosenthal! As in Sheridan Corporation?" Capone asked in disbelief. Rosenthal and Yatta's mother had been an on and off thing before and after Yatta was born. Rosenthal, a senator with ties to the political world, was believed to have participated in Yatta's murder conviction. Rosenthal was part owner of The Sheridan Corporation, a Fortune Five hundred company, and participated in numerous business ventures; the purchase of stocks and bonds was his specialty.

"How do you expect us to get to a nigga like that?" Capone asked.

"Let me worry about that," Key said.

"When you all get to him, Key knows what to do next. I got to deal with something else," Yatta said as he turned to leave.

***

Today was Vinny's wife's thirty-fourth birthday and he was about to throw a feast. He hired the best chef from Italy, rented a massive ballroom, and invited a host of family and friends. They all sat at a huge marble table while Vinny hurled jokes and gifts to everyone.

"Time for a toast," Vinny stood, tapping his champagne flute with a fork. A massive thunderstorm was brewing outside the ballroom. Bolts of lightning preceded thunderous roars that could bring down a lesser structure. "That was God raising his glass in unison," Vinny said jokingly. The room erupted in laughter. "Let's toast to family, friends, success, and my beautiful wife, who cost me nearly a million dollars spoiling her on this rainy day." Vinny continued with the jokes, yelling punch lines as he tried to speak over the claps of thunder that seemed to explode, causing the lights to go dark. "Everybody just remain calm," Vinny said. "The back up generators will kick in shortly."

When the lights came on, men wielding assault rifles surrounded the table. No one moved. "What the fuck is this?" Vinny yelled as he pulled himself up from the table.

"Have a seat Vinny," Anisa said as she walked into the ballroom. Anisa was dressed for the occasion in a custom-made Alexander McQueen dress. Her hair brushed past her shoulders. She held a bottle of Dom Perion in one hand and a gold, desert eagle in the other. As she approached the table, one of her men snatched a guest from his seat. Anisa took the seat and placed a napkin in her lap. "Vinny,Vinny, Vinny. You sure find ways to piss off the boss. While not an easy task, you've mastered it," Anisa said as she slid the bottle of Dom Perion to Vinny and filled her plate with pasta and meatballs.

"You got some balls coming here and disrespecting me in front of my family." Vinny's anger grew.

"Spicy, but good," Anisa said as she sampled the food. "Mona wishes you a Happy Birthday," Anisa said to Vinny's wife, pointing at her with a fork.

"You tell that bitch to go to hell," Vinny spat.

"So disrespectful," Anisa responded. "Look around. My men are dressed for the occasion; expensive Armani suits and ties. Their fucking ties are Armani. I never knew they made fucking ties."

"You struck a nerve this time Vinny, which is why I'm here. You set a meeting with her sons and she didn't like that."

"You're dead, fucking dead!" Vinny's brother, Tony, snapped at Anisa.

"You don't have any clue who you're dealing with." Anisa pointed her gun at Tony, but changed her mind. "I'm not going to shoot you," she said, rising from her seat and walking over to Tony. There was a large meat cleaver on the table. Anisa picked it up. "Put your hand on the table," Anisa ordered. Tony didn't comply. Anisa told one of her men to put a gun to Tony's wife's head. "Now, if you don't put your hand on the table, your wife's brains will be on the table instead." This time Tony complied.

"Since I believe in being fair, I'll let you choose which hand you want to keep. If I was you, I would prefer the hand you use the most." The guests looked at Anisa as if she was crazy. Tony pulled his right hand from the table and replaced it with his left hand. Anisa advised him that she would count to three. She did, but she swung the meat cleaver into Tony's skull. Guests filled the room with terrifying screams. Anisa calmly walked back to her seat.

"Now, back to you," Anisa said. "What would you do if you was Mona and had been disrespected?" Vinny starred at Anisa. "Okay, I see," Anisa said. She whispered to one of her men to shoot one of the guests in the head. Another body hit the floor. Anisa took a sip of her drink and asked the question again. "What would you do if you was Mona under these circumstances?" Vinny's lips moved but nothing came out.

"I didn't catch that. What did you say? Anisa asked.

"I said I would retaliate. I would blow her fucking house up."

"Now that wasn't so hard was it?" Anisa said as she got out of her chair. She then walked over to Vinny's wife who was crying and shaking. Anisa put her gun to the back of her head and whispered, "What's your name?"

"Stephanie. My name is Stephanie," she replied in a shaky tone.

"Open your eyes and watch your wife die," Anisa told Vinny.

"What do you want from me?" he asked in an angry but fearful tone.

"Tell your wife you love her," Anisa ordered. Vinny looked at Stephanie and said he loved her with the deepest conviction and sincerity he could muster. Anisa erupted into laughter. "You're a funny guy. That was hilarious. Did you see the look on his face?" Anisa asked one of the guests, who froze in silence. "I asked you a fucking question," she yelled at the man who was unable to answer the question. He then uttered a faint "yes," closed his eyes, waiting for a bullet to crash into his skull. Anisa held the gun to Stephanie's head and pulled the trigger. Her forehead exploded as brain fragments and blood coated the table. Vinny screamed and launched at Anisa. One of her men contained him.

"You're responsible for all of these peoples' lives. Their blood is on your hands," Anisa whispered to Vinny. "Kill everybody but Vinny!" Anisa yelled as she left the ballroom. The smell of gunfire and smoke filled the room. Vinny closed his eyes, allowing his anger to consume him, as pandemonium was everywhere. All lines had been crossed and Mona would feel his wrath. He vowed this to be the least of his fury.

It's better to meet a bear robbed of her cub, than to meet a fool in his folly…

"Let's Make A Deal."

Reno, Nevada
February 12, 2012
1:30 pm

Vino Arturo, age 30 and head of the Arturo Family, was one of the youngest members of The Sheridan Syndicate. Vino was a good-looking man. At five foot eleven inches, blue eyes and nicely groomed hair, he made a fine appearance. Wealth only added to his stature. His father once ran the family, but fell victim to betrayal. He turned informant for the Feds, promising to testify against Mona. Vino caught wind of the deception and killed his father. To show respect, Vino decapitated his father and delivered the head to Mona. His loyalty was never questioned as he ran the Arturo Family from that day forward.

Vino sped off in his Porch Panamera 911 as the top folded into the back of his car. The phone rang. "Mr. Arturo, this is Governor Perez. Sorry I'm just now contacting you. I had a hard time convincing the board to allow your permits to go through, but I managed."

"That's great news Governor, and rest assured, you won't regret it," Vino said as he pulled into an underground parking garage.

"Well, I have to go. We'll take this conversation up later over a game of golf."

"Sounds good Governor. You have a good day." Vino parked near a white van and stepped out. Two men emerged from the van and opened the back door. A badly beaten man struggled to stand. His name was Edgar, Vino's cousin. Edgar had been stealing from Vino for quite some time. At first it was small amounts, then he became greedy.

"You've got three seconds to tell me why I shouldn't kill you," Vino said as he removed his thousand dollar Loree Rodkin shades. The seconds passed. Vino took a gun from one of the men's waist and fired multiple shots into Edgar's body. "Time is money and money is time," Vino said, speeding away in his Porsche.

***

Hazel Crest, Illinois
February 16, 2012
11:57 pm

Peter Rosenthal was what most people called an opportunist and very perspicacious; insightful, a less educated man might say. Peter had touched all of the stepping-stones needed to reach the top of the food chain. He was in his mid-fifties and in good health.

The higher-ups stayed clear of Peter, trying not to provoke him. He had crossed so many people; damaged reputations; and managed to entrap high-ranking government officials committing treason, espionage, fraud, money laundering, and the selling of classified documents. The corruption went as high as The Pentagon and on up to the President's Cabinet. Peter received federal grants and other funds to help finance The Sheridan Corporation. His leverage over other people had served him well.

Peter walked to the garage and slid inside the car. As he reached to adjust the rear view mirror, he saw a figure in the back seat and felt the cold metal press against his neck. "I've got a few hundred dollars in my wallet and a twenty-thousand dollar Rolex. Take it," Peter said as he became agitated that he would be late to his meeting with an important woman. Peter looked hard at the intruder and smirked. "Look at you, all grown up now." Peter recognized Key and smiled.

"Put your hands on the steering wheel," Key ordered. Peter complied. Key, Capone, and Deno had spent the past two weeks searching for Peter. Key knew about Peter's condo in Hazel Crest.

"You're the messenger?" Peter asked. "All of these years and I bet Yatta still has no clue what you did, huh?"

"Shut up!" Key slammed her gun upside Peter's head. He was out cold.

***

Dallas, Texas
February 17, 2012
8:00 am

Mona and her sons sat across the table from Janice and Jasmine Lockhart. The Lockhart sisters were sole shareholders of Meddstone, a small drilling company. While Meddstone had gone through hard times and was on the brink of bankruptcy, Mona saw an opportunity to be seized. Her vision eventually turned Meddstone into a major company worth more than one hundred billion dollars.

"What's our production since converting to the new methods?" Ty asked the sisters. Mona made sure Ty and Sky learned the energy business.

"We're not focusing on nuclear electric power, so our medium in production is all in crude and petroleum material. The use of geothermal energy is a bit below average," Janice explained.

“And our methane and carbon dioxide levels are below average as well,” Jasmine added.

Ty asked about the clean energy projects. “The solar panels are in mass production as we speak and we’re using a lot of conventional hydro-electric power, and wind as well,” Jasmine replied.

“And that’s outside of natural gases?” Sky questioned.

“Correct,” Jasmine answered with certainty.

“Our only problem as of now is the drilling. Meddstone sits on a piece of property shared with a motorcycle club. We can’t drill until they give us legal consent to do so,” Janice explained.

“Have the trucks prepped and ready to drill by next week,” Mona said. “I’ll deal with the problem. Exxon Mobil is selling a drilling site located in the Pacific Ocean, guaranteed at least 2.3 billion barrels of oil. I think that’s something we should look into before BP takes the land.

“Yeah, I agree,” Jasmine replied. “Let’s have our people meet with theirs and go from there.” The meeting went a bit longer before everybody called it in and headed their separate ways.

***

Chicago, Illinois
February 17, 2012
9:06 pm

The warehouse windows were broken years ago, allowing the blizzard-like wind to cut into his skin like tiny needles. Cracks in the building’s foundation made whistling sounds as the winds swept out any lingering heat. The headlights of a truck pulling into the warehouse awakened Peter Rosenthal. Peter was taken against his will some twenty-four hours earlier. When the headlights went out, a group of people approached him.

"I don't know what my Mother saw in you," Yatta said as he sat at an old desk next to Peter. "You're about as crooked as they come."

"Welcome home," Peter jeered. "I would hug you, but I'm tied up at the moment. Where do we start since this is not a social visit?"

"The Sheridan Corporation," Yatta answered. "I want the corporate certificates -- the bonds, stocks, I want everything."

"You're kidding, right?" Peter said.

"Do I look like I'm kidding? You're tied up, not me. There's a blizzard coming. But you can stay here if you like. I'm sure no one would bother you," Yatta shot back. "I'm curious. Where's that son of yours?"

"I haven't seen Nate in years," Peter admitted.

"Why did you set me up?" Yatta asked. "I spent every night thinking about it and never came close to understanding why."

"There's a lot of things you don't know about people," Peter said as he looked at Key.

"Just let me kill him and get it over with," Key snapped. Yatta told her to chill. Peter smiled a pleasant grin.

"You think shits funny, huh?" Yatta inquired.

"I can see the humor in the most awkward abominable situations that may occur," Peter said, still making light of the situation. Yatta told Capone to give him the photos. Capone and Deno had kidnapped his wife and two daughters. Peter cherished his children, always keeping them out of harms way. As Peter looked at the pictures, his mood went from humorous, to scared and uncomfortable.

"What happened to the humor?" Yatta said with a slight smile on his face.

"You can't run or sell anything that's tied to The Sheridan Corporation. Not without the approval of my silent partner," Peter explained.

"Let me worry about that," Yatta replied.

"You have no idea who you're dealing with. We're not talking about some street level thugs," Peter warned.

"Where is your son?" Yatta asked, ignoring his warning.

"He's in Rochester, New York. When you kill him, tell him disloyalty always catches up to you." Yatta smiled at the comment. "Father like son." Yatta cut Peter loose.

"Here's the deal. You make the paperwork appear under a name I give you. Don't contact your silent partner. Once you transfer the deed of ownership, you'll get your family back. You contact anyone about our arrangements – you get the picture?" Yatta headed for his truck. Peter knew this would probably cost him his life; rather him than his family.

"Sex And Violence In A Place Called Home."

Minneapolis, Minnesota
February 25, 2012
10:07 pm

Family is the most important thing in this world. It's the motivation that separates the man from the streets and the man at home. A man's woman is his most prized possession, giving him reason to return each day. If you destroy his family and the place he calls home, you'll experience the purest side of evil.

Natasha – dark complexion, brown eyes, five foot five inches, and a body built for lustful intentions – held the fragrance of freshly picked roses. Tasha, as she liked to be called, belonged to Yatta. They had a son, Lil J -- eighteen and on his way to college. Tasha and Yatta shared an understanding that most would not appreciate. Yatta kept his street life separate from Tasha and Lil J. Even if that meant barely coming home, that was the price he was willing to pay. Tasha understood his absence and supported him no matter what.

Yatta surprised Tasha by flying home. Lil J was over at a friend's house spending the night. While Yatta and Tasha had not been together since their teenage years, they maintained their love for each other throughout his incarceration. The two of them enjoyed the evening and caught up on the important things that had transpired over the previous weeks. When Yatta looked over his shoulder, Tasha was asleep. They had retired to the couch to watch a movie.

The morning sun shined bright onto Tasha's face, waking her from a deep sleep. Yatta made breakfast and drove Lil J to school.

"Come in," she said, soaking in the tub. Yatta sat down with his back against the tub.

"I made a move against Peter Rosenthal last week. I got control of The Sheridan Corporation and I'm set to meet with the silent partner." Tasha sometimes helped Yatta think through things whenever he was unsure of himself. He trusted her with his life.

"What's your end game?" she said.

"I'm going to sell the shares of stocks that Peter owned to the silent partner. I can use the money to invest in something else."

"You think Peter's just going to roll over and let you get away with this?"

"Honestly, I'm not sure," Yatta said.

"You got to kill him Yatta." He knew she was right

"Enough business talk, I need some chocolate," Yatta said as he quickly undressed. As he climbed into the tub, Tasha turned the other way to face him. She put her feet on his chest. Yatta began to suck her toes.

"Let's go to the bedroom," Yatta said as he lifted her from the tub. Once in the bed, he wasted no time. He inserted his penis into her folds. Her knuckles turned white as she grabbed hold of the red, satin sheets. Tasha's mound was nicely shaven and wet. She begged him to fuck her harder.

"Ooooohhh – yeah, just like that," she moaned in pleasure. She was so tight and wet that Yatta had to fight from exploding. "Fuccckkk, fuck me," she hissed through clenched teeth.

Yatta had spent so many nights in prison fantasying about this act. He no longer had to imagine it. He pushed deeper and deeper. Tasha held her stomach.

"Shit, I can feel you inside my stomach." The combination of pain and pleasure was both mind-boggling and perplexing. Her moans made him quicken his pace and pound harder.

"Harder – please fuck me harder." She bit down on her bottom lip so hard she nearly drew blood. "Asssggghh…Ummh…umph – yeah!" Tasha screamed in ecstasy as she met his every sexual advance. Yatta turned Tasha onto her stomach and pulled her by the waist until she was on her knees. He slowly penetrated her and slammed into her wetness until she called for submission. They both came, collapsing onto the bed.

"I love you," Yatta said as he headed to the shower.

You can get lost in the realms of false perception and reality – all while living in the present moment. Nobody can predict the future or rewrite the past. Most of the time, you find yourself at adversity when it comes to making decisions. The illusion of the truth wears a mask of deception, and deceit comes in many forms of truth…

***

Ty's estate in Arizona was his getaway, offering solitude from his family and friends. Ty demanded the finest amenities for his retreat; a golf course, indoor swimming pool, full-sized basketball and tennis courts. Italian leather recliners and expensive carpet adorned the wooden floors, and paintings by Luca Della Robbis, Giovanni Cimabue, and Lucas Cranach decorated the walls.

Ty's personal assistant, Olivia Green, greeted him. She had supported Ty for the past five years. "How did things go at the shareholders meeting?" she asked.

"Good, but we need to deal with a property line situation. I'm dog tired," Ty said, collapsing on the sofa. Olivia sat next to him and smiled. The two got along well.

"You're going to work yourself to death."

"What's on my schedule?" Ty asked while his eyes were closed.

"Surprisingly, you're free of work," Olivia replied. Ty hid the ugly nature of the business from Olivia, but she wasn't any fool. She was thirty-years old, honey-brown eyes, and hair that hung well below her shoulders. Olivia stood five feet, six inches, sporting a petite frame. She took pride in her appearance.

Ty never fathomed the thought of hiring a stranger to work for him and keep track of his personal life, but he couldn't resist her charm. She was very down to earth and easy to get along with.

"What do you want to do?" Ty asked, catching her off guard.

"What do you mean?"

"For fun. What do you do for fun? You said I had some free time, so let's use it." Olivia thought long and hard.

"Laser tag. Let's go play laser tag," she said, beaming with excitement.

Ty's phone rang. He told Olivia to give him a second. "Sky, what's up bro?"

"We got hit in West Virginia. The money is the least of our worries. We had some important documents in the safe that got lifted," Sky explained.

"Shit!" Ty said, sitting to attention. "Who do you think was behind this?"

"From what I was told – The Dominicans. But I know The Cuadras Cartel had their hands in it. The deeds to the docks for that region were in that safe," Sky vented.

"Mona hear about this?"

"Naw, not yet," Sky replied.

"Let's deal with this first before we tell her. Have Kema meet me out there," Ty said, ending the call.

"Is everything alright?" Olivia asked.

"One of our locations got robbed. I've got to fly out immediately," Ty replied. "I need you to call and have the jet fueled and ready to go. Rain check on the laser tag," he added.

"Of course – business first." As Olivia made the calls, Ty closed his eyes and considered his next move.

"Do I Hear An Amen?"

Rochester, New York
March 1, 2012
2:16 pm

"Let the Church say Amen!" Nate yelled, feeling the Holy Ghost surging within his body. He made all of the changes necessary to move on with his life. Nate felt that God had a plan for him, giving him a profound purpose.

Nate's story could be a testimony worth voicing. In his heart, he believed God already had a place in heaven for him, and he was prepared to serve One Master and One Master only – God, his Almighty Kingdom. "God is Good!" Nate continued to preach.

"I remember being lost in that death culture, caught in the grasp of madness that the streets offered," Nate shared. "God pulled me from the depths of despair and granted me salvation; true peace and tranquility." The congregation of The Church stood and clapped as Nate gave his electrifying sermon. Although he was just an Assistant Minister, the people found life in his words.

"No matter what life threw my way, God made sure I caught it and found favor in the decisions I made. God never gave up, no matter how bad the decision. His light keeps shinning on me. I was lost and caught in the snares of death. He…" Nate paused and pointed to the sky. "He saved me, resurrected me, and gave me back my life," Nate said as tears ran down his face.

After the service, he shook hands and said his goodbyes. Nate spoke briefly with the Head Pastor, and then retired to his studies for a prayer with God.

While wrapped up in prayer, he felt a breeze blow in from the window. Nate never opened the window in his office, wondering who could've opened it. He turned and saw Key sitting on his desk. Nate smiled a peaceful grin and put his hands together in prayer. (Nate and Chuck were longtime enemies of Yatta. Key was sent to settle the score.)

"Prayer won't help you out of this," Key said, pointing her weapon at Nate.

"I'm not praying for me," Nate said. "It's for you." Having said that, Key unloaded her magazine, making certain he was dead.

Why believe in God and sacrifice your life, when he'll let you die and not guard yours…

***

Charleston, West Virginia
March 1, 2012
10:37 pm

Nora was a Dominican who made a living robbing safe houses and sticking people up. He had men who handled themselves well and completed ever job they targeted. They recently hit a real estate office and pulled out a six-foot cast iron safe. That was the easy part. Getting it open was the challenge. Nora called Jessie, a man experienced in cracking high-end safes. As soon as Jessie found out whom the safe belonged to he contacted Sky and told him what he knew. Jessie then called Nora and told him to sit tight. He would be right over.

"Yo, that shit was mad crazy son. I was fucking that bitch while her dude was watching," Nora bragged to his homies.

"Where this nigga at yo. I want to see what's in this safe," one of Nora's men said.

Just then there was a knock at the door. Nora got up and went to check who was there. "Who is it?" Nora asked.

"It's me, Corey. You called me about the safe." Nora opened the door. Kema's men rushed the apartment and put everybody on the floor. Kema and Ty were the last to walk in. Kema locked the door behind them. Ty took a seat on the couch and removed his shades.

"There was a safe stolen from my property and I want it back. But first, I want the man responsible for taking it. Who is Nora?" Ty asked. No body answered him. Ty then looked at Kema and she went to work. Kema squatted next to the man closest to her.

"Where is Nora?" she asked politely.

"Fuck you!" The man spat. Kema blew his brains across the floor.

"Where is Nora?" She asked the next man.

"I don-…" Kema put a bullet in his head before he could finish his sentence.

"Where – is Nora?" She asked again and this time followed the frightened man's eyes and found Nora.

"Snatch him up," Kema ordered one of her men. Nora was pinned against the wall and Ty approached him.

"So, you're the one who got my safe?" Ty asked, looking him dead in the face.

"It's in the back room," Nora said. Ty went to check the safe and to his surprise, everything was there. He had his men empty the safe. He then went to deal with Nora.

“You stole from me. What should I do?” Ty asked.

“Yo, you ain’t got to worry about me dawg – word,” Nora replied.

“Good! Throw him out the window,” Ty ordered. Nora was thrown through the window structure onto the concrete pad some twenty-feet below.

“Let’s go,” Ty said.

“What about the rest of them?” One of the men asked about the other Dominicans.

Kema took his assault rifle, slaughtered them and then gave the rifle back to him.

“Let’s go,” Kema said. They left the court-way building with the contents in the safe.

***

Reno, Nevada
March 3, 2012
1:19 pm

“What do you think about golf, son?” Governor Perez asked Vino. Governor Perez was a capitalist who played both sides of the fence. He had ties linked to the Italian mobs that ran the Nevada casinos. While his political clout kept him untouchable, he was a crook by any meaning of the word.

“Not much Governor. I’m not big on the sport,” Vino admitted.

“Your father was a man of integrity and character. He had big values and morals that I appreciate. Are you like your father?” The Governor inquired.

“Me and my father are two different kinds of animals, Governor. He was satisfied with catching fish of small caliber. I chase the whales and sharks. But being that he was the man that raised me, we do share similar qualities,” Vino spoke firmly.

"Let's talk golf. A birdie is a score of one stroke under par for the hole, and a bogey is a score of one stroke over par for the hole. There's a whole lot to learn about this game," Governor Perez explained. He swung the golf club and then pulled an envelop from his back pocket. "Don't forget our arrangements," he said, passing the envelop to Vino.

"We all have rules that governs our actions. Our arrangements are a contract. Just as I can assure you things will hold up on my end, I expect the same from you," Vino explained.

"The last thing I wish to do would be to piss Mona off. That woman has neither compassion nor consideration of decency. Hell, if you knew better, you would run away and put some distance between you and that woman," the Governor warned.

You lay with dogs, you'll wake up with fleas, and most dogs got fleas…

Bridgewater Penitentiary To The Royal Diamond Casino & Resort

San Antonio, Texas
Bridgewater Penitentiary
March 4, 2012
8:00 am

"In this world, you live by a set of rules and principles that not only governs your longevity in the underworld, but also shapes who you are as a player in the game of chances," Mona explained as she sat across the table from Gator, the Founder of the White Lion Motor Cycle Gang. They sold meth, guns, counterfeit currency, and ran the Texas highways and interstates. Gator was known as an honorable and respected man throughout Texas. At six foot eight inches, two-hundred-sixty-pounds of muscle, he was a massive, intimidating man. Gator was currently serving a six-year prison sentence for carrying a concealed weapon and aggravated assault. He hurled a policeman over his police cruiser and beat him unconscious. Gator ran Bridgewater State Penitentiary and experienced no problem getting what he needed into the prison. His only problem was Warden Reed who was trying to get Gator transferred to a more secured prison where Gator wouldn't have as much influence.

Gator thought long and hard before he answered. He knew who Mona was and understood the stature she possessed. Respect was everything – even if that meant dying for it. "I understand those principles and I live by them same codes," Gator finally spoke.

"I think we both can help each other under these circumstances, without strong arming the other. I run a company called…"

"Meddstone," Gator interjected. "Your land and drilling sites sits on a piece of our property. I'm familiar with who you are."

"You see, my trucks can't start to drill without the consent of the owners of that land," Mona explained. "I understand you have a problem with Warden Reed. Is that correct?"

"She knows she can't control me nor stop the things I have going on in this prison. So, she's trying to get me sent further up state," Gator explained.

Mona pulled out her cellphone and called the Warden. When Warden Reed picked up, Mona put the phone on speaker. "I'm sitting across from a Mr. Jason Strathorn. I need you to cancel your plans to send him out of this facility."

"Mona, I can't…"

"Warden Reed, that wasn't a request. You do what you have to do, but Mr. Strathorn is to stay put." Mona hung up. When Mona said her farewell to Gator, he looked on in amazement. He'd never met a person – let alone a woman -- who had so much power.

***

Reno, Nevada
March 7, 2012
9:00 pm

Today was the grand opening of The Royal Diamond Casino and Resort. Together, Vino, Ty, and Sky made their investors happy, and in return, impressed Mona. Now, with the permits from the Gambling commissioner, The Royal Diamond Casino and Resort was a full operational business open to the public.

Everybody came out for the grand opening and dressed accordingly. Even Mona, who avoided the press core and flashing cameras on the red carpet, sported a one hundred thousand dollar dress and matching stilettos designed by Torri Forney. Her neck was wrapped in diamonds and her hair was elegantly styled. Anisa and Kema dressed down in matching Dolce and Gabanna dresses as they led Mona through the crowd of people. Ty and Sky were playing host and welcoming their guests.

"To The Royal Diamond!" Vino said as they all retired to the banquet room and raised their campaign glasses in unison.

"I've got to admit it, you all did an outstanding job making this come alive," Mona said as she gave props to her comrades.

"This is just the beginning. Our next project will be in Vegas – open a second Casino and continue to make power moves," Sky chimed in.

"Well, I got to hit the floors and do some mingling with the people who come to spend their money," Vino said, leaving the room.

"We can clean twice the amount of bills we're cleaning now," Ty said.

"That's always a plus, but for now – we're not going to use this venture to launder anything. Let's allow it to generate it's own cash flow. Then use that capital and reinvest, launder the bills from our investment margins," Mona explained.

While Mona was talking to her sons, she noticed Anisa's concern as she followed Carlos and his entourage. Anisa looked at Mona for permission to engage, but Mona had other plans. "Invite your friends up," Mona said. Kema and Anisa searched Carlos and brought him into the V.I.P. section.

"Wow!" This place is nice." Carlos complimented as he took a seat across from Mona. Sky shot daggers at him and Ty had a blank expression on his face.

"What brings you here?" Mona inquired.

"I come to support an old friend," Carlos said with a smirk on his face.

"You're a ravishing woman. After all these years, you're still beautiful and full of youth," Carlos added.

"Everybody out!" Mona said, while looking Carlos in the eyes. Anisa saw to it that Carlos' men made their exit first, then filing out the room with hers and standing guard at the door. Mona grabbed two glasses and put three ice cubes in each. After preparing the drinks, Mona took her seat and slid Carlos a drink. "You got my attention – talk!" Mona said.

"I would be the first to admit that Vinny can be quite provoking and unintelligent. But you killed a lot of good people at that gathering. Stephanie was a sweet young lady…"

"Wrong place, wrong time," Mona said cutting him off.

"How long do you expect this war to last – honestly?" Carlos inquired.

"My Syndicate is worth more than a hundred billion dollars in capital. I can war as long as your men willing to die," Mona replied with clarity.

"You've always been cocky, but not too willing to compromise. My son's an estranged man now, that you killed his wife. So, he's unpredictable," Carlos said as he stood to leave. But Mona called out to him.

"How do you know I'm going to let you leave here tonight?" Mona asked

"Killing me with my guard down isn't your M.O.? You like the sport of being challenged. You like to toy with your adversaries first. Besides we're good friends. Friends don't kill friends."

"And you were always so naïve. I'll send you Vinny in a pine crate."

"Make it a wooden one and I'll bury him," Carlos said, leaving Mona to herself.

Anisa walked in with Kema. "What do you want us to do?" Anisa asked.

"Enjoy the night!" Mona said as she left the V.I.P. section.

When blood spills, somebody has to clean it up...

***

Yatta sat at the table and went over the last of the signed documents that Peter Rosenthal had sent him. The Sheridan Corporation was worth more than Yatta suspected. The Sheridan acted as venture capitalist for Meddstone Drilling Company and The Royal Diamond Casino and Resort. Both entities combined for a hundred and fifty billion dollars net worth.

Yatta was enroute to meet with the silent partners at The Sheridan Corporation headquarters. He and Capone were the only ones that would attend the meeting. Yatta brought Capone along because he had a degree in business management and corporate construction assessment.

"Yo, you trust these people? How you know they not going to call the twist and get us locked the fuck up?" Capone asked Yatta as he drove to the location listed.

"I don't, but Peter is as crooked as any man I know. I don't see him playing no police games," Yatta assured him.

Capone pulled up to a large building and parked. They were dressed casually, carrying brief cases in their hands. While they were on the elevator going up, Capone made light of their attire. "We're a long way from the projects my nigga. Good thing my elocutions up to par and I can converse like the educated brother from the bank," Capone joked.

Once the doors opened, they found themselves in an office. Capone saw a beautiful woman sitting on a desk while another woman sat in the chair. As they walked pass the doorway, there was a third beautiful woman leaning against the wall. "Have a seat. I'm Mona Moore." Yatta and Capone took their seats and Anisa took a seat as well. "Why are you here?" Mona asked.

"I'm the sole controller of..." Anisa began laughing.

"You don't even sound like you belong here. Let's cut the act and be frank," Mona said. Yatta and Capone were both caught off guard.

"I think we should reschedule this meeting," Yatta suggested, standing ready to leave.

"I insist we move forward," Mona said.

"I don't think that I'm willing to sell any more," Yatta said as a matter of fact. As they started to leave, Anisa and Kema pulled out guns and told them to have a seat. Both men complied.

"Apparently you don't know who I am but we're past that. The documents you acquired, you're going to return them to their rightful owner," Mona explained.

"What if that's not an option?" Capone asked.

Mona laughed. "Listen, I'm not asking you to turn over what you stole. You are going to. That's not up for debate. Yatta, you have a girl friend and a son that lives in Minnesota and Capone, your mother is in a nursing home in Ohio. I can tell your every move you made for the last two weeks. I could kill you both right now. Don't try my patience," Mona explained. The things she knew surprised Yatta. They both used fake names and she still dug things up on them.

"I'll contact you at a later time," Mona said, walking towards the elevator.

"Consider you're the lucky one," Anisa said to Yatta as she left the office.

Blood In The Water

Miami, Florida
March 12, 2012
11:17 pm

Ty owned a luxury boat company named Sail, a business outside of The Sheridan Syndicate that specialized in yachts and speedboats. Today he finished the inventory for new boats that arrived from Germany. It was unusual for him to stay this late, but he needed to check every boat for any defects.

While Ty stood in the parking lot, he noticed a van parked next to his Porsche. That's when he saw a hooded man run behind a brick pillar. Ty knew he had to get to his car to retrieve his gun. Ty heard footsteps behind him. He turned around quickly – nothing. Ty hit the trunk magnetism from his keypad that unlocked the trunk. He tossed the briefcase in his trunk and grabbed his handgun. Ty surveyed the parking lot and saw nothing. Then all hell broke loose. The hooded man emerged and let off a couple shots. Another gunman shot from the opposite side of the parking lot. Ty ducked for cover. They were trying to pin him down.

The doors on the van next to his car opened. Two gunmen jumped out. Ty fired under the car, hitting one of them. He then crawled around the car and killed him. Ty felt hot metal rip through his shoulder, turned and fired multiple shots into the dark night. As Ty struggled to stand, he was hit again, causing him to fall to the ground. The shooter kicked the gun away from Ty, squatted, took off his hood and looked into his eyes.

"Vinny sends his regards," the man said. Ty spit blood in the man's face. The sounds of incoming police sirens grew as the man stood and pointed his gun at Ty's head. After pulling the trigger, the man sat a bottle of Dom Perion next to Ty's lifeless body and drove away.

***

Langley, Virginia
March 17, 2012
8:30 pm

"Agent Kemp, what's the status on moving forward with the raid?" Shaw, the Director of the C.I.A. inquired.

"As of now, my intel is solid, but not so much against Mona Moore. So, to push for a raid now would due her no harm. The only families we could tie down are the Stein and Arturo Families. Mona made sure nothing illegal could be tied to her or her family," Agent Kemp explained.

Kemp had infiltrated The Sheridan Syndicate. Although she had been working undercover for some five years, the things she learned about The Syndicate were limited.

"We're expending too many resources on this matter. We need to make more progress." Mr. Shaw shared his concern about Agent Kemp's work.

"I haven't had the chance to be around Mona or hear her speak about anything in person. She's very careful about what she says, and the people around her," Agent Kemp replied.

"Sir, I think we should grant Agent Kemp more time to infiltrate into the Syndicate," Cynthia Davis said. Cynthia was the Assistant Director of the C.I.A. "Besides, we have never gotten in this deep. Maybe Kemp can gain trust from the family and work herself into the conversations said behind closed doors."

"Our taxpayer's money isn't endless. But due to the nature of this case and all of its complications, I will give Agent Kemp additional time to proceed – but not forever," Shaw said as he left the room.

Once it was all clear, Cynthia Davis made a call. "You have the Director ready to move against Mona. I bought her more time, but I'm afraid I won't be able to stop the next raid. You guys have a mole in your organization."

"Who is it?" Anisa asked.

"That information is highly classified. Only the Director and me have access to that data. If I tell you who, I would be going to a prison cell."

"I'll be in touch," Anisa said, ending the call.

"Shit!" Cynthia Davis said, running her fingers through her hair.

Poker isn't a game that requires you to be skilled with the cards, but being able to bluff and hope your hand doesn't get called…

***

Miami, Florida
March 21, 2012
1:37 pm

"How long has he been like this?" Mona asked the doctor who performed the surgery on Ty.

"Almost two weeks. He has a lot of swelling around the brain and has lost a lot of blood. I will monitor him closely, making certain the swelling doesn't increase. He's lucky to be alive – he took a bullet to the head." Ty was heavily medicated and in an induced coma. The doctor put his hand on Mona's shoulder then walked off. Mona was enraged and filled with fury. The attempt on her son's life was the ultimate sign of disrespect. Ty was found unconscious in the parking lot when the police arrived at the scene. By the time he made it to the hospital, he had died. But the doctors managed to resuscitate him. Mona made arrangements to have security around Ty's room twenty-four hours a day.

Olivia rushed into Ty's room. "I'm sorry I couldn't get here earlier. I caught a flight right away. How is he?" she asked.

"He's not dead and that's all we can ask for at this moment," Mona said as she left the room. Mona trusted that Olivia would do right by Ty's family. There weren't many things that Mona was emotionally attached to in this world, but a mother's attachment to the lives she brought into this world is unimaginable.

***

Chicago, Illinois
March 24, 2012
3:16 am

Judge Posner was sleeping when Yatta found his bedroom. While Yatta was going through the names that Peter Rosenthal had blackmailed and used for his own personal gains, he saw Judge James L. Posner; the same judge that presided over the trial leading to Yatta's conviction.

Yatta turned the lights on, waking Judge Posner up. Seeing a stranger dressed in black frightened the judge. "How did you get into my home? Get the hell out right now before I call the police." Yatta ignored his rants and took a seat. He placed the gun across his lap and tossed the judge some bank statements.

"You of all people should know who I am. You're the one who sentenced me to prison. You also received two payments of half a million dollars from Peter Rosenthal. What a coincidence!" Yatta explained.

"Honey, turn the lights out wh…" Posner's wife sat up and saw Yatta. "Honey, what's going on?" She asked in a worried tone.

"It's alright," the judge said, trying to console her.

"Answer my question!" Yatta yelled.

"I'm calling the cops," the judge said as he reached for the phone. Yatta snatched it from his hand and shot his wife in the shoulder.

"Aaaaggghhh!" She bellowed in pain.

"You can answer my questions and get her some help, or you can procrastinate and let her die – you choose."

"All I know is, I was assigned to your case by my superiors. I got a call from Peter, advising me that I had to convict you – no matter what. That's all I know."

"You're still lying," Yatta said as he pointed the gun at his wife.

"Okay, okay. He was protecting the girl. He never told me her name. All I know is he was protecting some girl," the judge admitted. Yatta was taken back; more confused than ever.

"What the fuck are you talking about – what girl?"

"I'm an associate judge – I wasn't elected into the position. My superiors were involved somehow. They gave me a set of instructions to follow and that's what I did."

"You never had this conversation with me," Yatta said. He then showed the judge that he recorded their conversation on his phone. "You say a word about this to anyone. This recording will go viral," Yatta assured him.

"We won't speak a word of it," the judge's wife said. Yatta stared at the judge and left as he came.

Confession Gone Bad

Havana, Cuba
March 31, 2012
11:00 am

Victoria was Carlos' wife and Vinny's mother – a devoted Catholic, a true believer in God. While she did not approve of their illicit activities, she stayed because of her love for Carlos. But things changed when her brother got himself killed, driving her mother to an early grave. Victoria gathered the courage to leave and never look back, and moved to Havana, Cuba where she opened a flower shop.

At 49, Victoria was beautiful and full of life; earth-green eyes and long dark hair accompanied by a peaceful energy. It was your typical warm day in Havana; a good time for her daily trip to the Cathedral for Holy Communion. She enjoyed confession, sharing the misery she had witnessed; a cleansing experience she felt, allowing her to become closer to God.

"Confess before the presence of the Lord," the Priest said.

"I've seen my husband kill people and I never intervened with the evil things he taught my son. I should have stood up for my son and helped him choose a better path, but I didn't." Her voice trembled with emotions.

"Some things are beyond our control," the Priest said. "You can't fault yourself for other peoples' past actions."

"I know, I'm not directly responsible for their actions, but I feel as if I could have prevented some things from happening."

"Remain pure at heart and God will not judge you for the acts of others. Say three Hail Marys and repent." To Victoria's surprise, the curtain pulled back and the devil appeared. It was Anisa, Mona's enforcer and archenemy of Carlos. Victoria did not confess to the Priest. She had confessed to Anisa.

What followed was the muffled sound of four bullets shot through a silencer. **Psst! Psst! Psst! Psst!** Anisa exited the confessional booth, snatched the holy veil from her neck, and left the Cathedral with no remorse for her actions. This was her job.

If you cross a bridge, expect the possibilities of it collapsing and you drowning. If you play with fire, expect flames. Nobody suffocates intentionally, but their actions can cause a lack of oxygen needed to breath – then they suffocate involuntarily...

***

Chicago, Illinois
April 1, 2012
1:36 am

The rain and wind were strong that night. Outdoor debris slammed against the house. Distant sounds of thunder grew, accompanied by intense lightning that filled the sky. A thunderous roar woke Yatta and knocked the power out. With all the things going on in Yatta's life, he had not been sleeping well. He struggled piecing together his past.

> *Yatta got out of bed and headed to the kitchen for a drink. While walking through the living room he couldn't see anyone, but felt like somebody was there. He blinked his eyes, trying to adjust to the darkness. Suddenly,*

something struck him over the head. He was out cold. He gradually regained his consciousness while rubbing the back of his head.

"You fouled out of the game." Yatta recognized the voice. It was Peter's. "You shouldn't have gone digging for things that were buried," Peter said, raising his gun. Yatta wasn't scared. He damn sure wasn't going to give Peter the pleasures of hearing him beg for his life. Peter pulled the trigger. The first shot sent Yatta crashing to the floor, gasping for air. The second shot pierced his skull. As Yatta began to fade, Peter placed the gun close to Yatta's head, making sure the final shot killed him.

Yatta woke from his nightmare in a cold sweat; his heart pumped fast. He went to the bathroom to wet his face, and then moved to the living room where he found Deno and Capone going over The Sheridan documents.

"Y'all up late. Where's Key? Yatta asked.

"She left a few hours ago to see some chick named Keyanna," Capone said. Yatta walked back to his room, hoping to find some peace.

***

Juarez, Mexico
April 5, 2012
1:45 pm

Vinny walked to the warehouse and found Carlos and some of his men sitting near a wooden crate. Carlos was pale, looking as if he was sick. "Have a seat," Carlos said to his son.

"Is everything alright? Why are we here in Mexico?" Vinny asked, taking a seat next to the wooden crate. Carlos ignored his question.

"You're my son and I love you. Truly, I do. But in this world we must take actions that are deemed necessary to survive; even if that requires the ultimate sacrifice."

"Father, I'm confused. Where are you going with this?"

"I had a talk with Mona," Carlos said.

"You had a talk with Mona?" Vinny asked with surprise. "You understand she killed my wife, friends, and family members. And you had a talk with her?" Vinny said. His voice rose in anger as he detected his father's lack of consideration.

"You see this crate that's sitting next to me? Well, if you don't, let me tell you a story about how it got here," Carlos spoke with a degree of sarcasm. "I had a conversation with Mona and she advised me that I would find you in a wooden crate. You made an attempt on her son's life?"

"Blood in this culture is only repaid in blood. You, my father, told me that."

"Yeah, well you're not fucking dead!" Carlos grew enraged as he pushed the top off of the wooden crate. When Vinny saw his mother he collapsed, tears running from his eyes.

"You're supposed to be the one in this fucking crate, not Victoria!" Carlos snapped as he pointed to the crate. Devastated and angered in his grief, Vinny cried over the death of his mother.

"You made the wrong call and this was the result," Carlos said as he again pointed to Victoria. "They sent me my wife in a fucking crate!"

As Vinny began to speak, one of the men put a plastic bag over his head. Another man hit Vinny in the stomach, causing him to gasp for air. Carlos couldn't watch; closed his eyes, waiting for it to be over. Vinny clawed at the attacker's hands, his life faded and fell limp. The attacker let go.

"Boss, it's done!" The man said.

"Put his body in the freezer," Carlos said. "Now I got two people to bury instead of one.

Its walls are patrolled day and night against invaders but the real danger is wickedness within the city…

"Calamity Engulfs You Like A Storm."

Casper, Wyoming
April 7, 2012
2:39 pm

Peter had an estate in Casper, Wyoming primarily used as a vacation spot and a sometimes-getaway; nine bedrooms, exercise room, spa, theater, and swimming pool. Peter left Chicago the week he signed over his ownership in The Sheridan Corporation to Yatta in exchange for his family.

Peter heard the security alarm beep, indicating a door was opened. Although he was alone, Peter sensed someone was in the house. He rushed to his safe to get his handgun, but was too late.

"Sit down," Yatta said.

"I see you're good at making interruptions. Haven't you got enough from me already?" Peter said as he took a seat.

"Why did you pay Judge Posner to sabotage my trial?" Yatta asked.

"Let's not go digging up old dirt. You're better off leaving some things unanswered."

"I'll be the judge of that. Talk," Yatta said, pointing his gun at Peter's head.

"You're in over your head and can't see the road ahead of you. There are some things that I'm unwilling to go into and this is one of them. So, you can shoot me if you want. You have bigger problems," he added.

"What the fuck you talking about?" Yatta asked, feeling a bit confused.

"The Sheridan property – the silent partner is a woman you wouldn't want any quarrel with. Her name is Mona – Mona Moore. She runs The Sheridan Syndicate and her reach could touch God and knock him from His Throne. And her girls, let me tell you. You wouldn't want Anisa or Kema on your trail." While Yatta didn't appear overly concerned, Mona sounded as if she wasn't to be fucked with.

"Who is this girl you're protecting?" Yatta asked, referring to the girl Judge Posner mentioned.

"How did you know about the girl?" Peter wanted to know. "Don't go digging for things you shouldn't dig up," Peter added

"You know," Yatta said. "I had a dream in which you said the same thing to me, right before you killed me. Now look at the advantage."

"You have secrets in your camp. I think you should start there," Peter suggested.

"Stop the riddles," Yatta demanded. "I'm here for answers."

"Well, let's start with K…" Peter said as he was hit with three bullets.

Psst!

Psst!

Psst!

Peter was coughing up blood from his neck. Yatta bent down, trying to locate the shooter. He pulled Peter behind the couch, listening to what Peter was trying to say. Yatta then sat him up. "My, my safe deposit box, get t..." Peter said.

Psst!

Psst!

Two slugs opened Peter's skull. Yatta knew from the shot sequence that there was a sniper shooting from the outside. He slowly backed out of the living room, and away from the house.

***

New York, New York
April 10, 2012
2:30 pm

It was common practice for Kema to accompany Sky on business trips. Mona insisted that one of the enforcers travel with her sons. After all, Ty was lying in some hospital fighting for his life. Sky and Kema arrived in New York City for business. Since they arrived several hours early, there was time to lounge around in the hotel. Sky was in a funk since his brother had been assaulted.

Sky dozed off and awakened several minutes later. He got up and walked to the bathroom. When he opened the door, Kema just stepped out of the shower. Sky was momentarily shocked, frozen in place. Seeing Kema naked made his mouth water with anticipation. She made no attempt to cover up.

"I'll be out in a minute," Kema said, starting to dry off. Sky moved closer to her. Kema stepped back. "Sky, what are you doing?" Kema asked in slight protest. Sky said nothing while he allowed his lips to brush against her. "We can't do this," Kema said as she felt her heart pounding.

"You don't have to. I'll do it for the both of us," Sky replied as he picked her up and sat her on the sink.

Kema's skin was resplendent and soft; her wet hair and green eyes grabbed his attention as Sky ogled her with a deep desire. Kema felt his erection growing; balling her toes and giving into his advances. While Kema knew she was crossing a line, she wanted to breathe some life back into Sky. And if that meant sacrificing her body, that was okay.

Kema hadn't been with a man in some time; forgot how it felt to be pleased and devoured in pleasure. She reached down, undid his pants and removed his clothes. Sky pulled his shirt off, kissed her while placing his fingers inside her folds. Kema tensed up, digging her nails into his back. Sky kissed her lips while placing his erection inside of her; slowly, pushing his entire length into her wetness. Kema arched her back as their strides picked up in unison. She then pulled at his waist, encouraging him to fuck her harder. Kema made the adjustments needed to accommodate the thickness of his shaft. Her legs were propped up. Sky was pounding her with long strokes as she grew wetter. Her eyes seemed to roll up into the back of her head. A thick white substance from her vagina coated his erection with her natural lubricant.

"Let's go to the couch," Kema said, walking out of the bathroom. Once they made it to the couch, Kema bent over and Sky guided himself into her folds. Kema threw herself back, challenging his every sexual advance. She reached back, pulling her ass cheeks apart so he could dig inside her with deeper strokes. While Sky pounded harder and harder, Kema didn't budge. They both came as the pleasure was uncontrollable. The two of them lay in silence, waiting while their emotions calmed. Kema then headed to the bathroom saying, "Let's not make things awkward between us. We still got to work together."

***

Reno, Nevada
April 17, 2012
4:15 pm

As Vino walked out of his daughter's school, he held her over his head. Amber was his youngest daughter at age nine. Brittany, the oldest, was eleven. Vino loved his daughters more than life its self, giving them the best things money could buy.

"Daddy, Daddy, can we get some ice cream?" Amber asked. "Pretty, pretty, pretty please?" Amber added with a puppy-dog look.

"Last one to the truck is a rotten egg," Vino said as he began to run. When they arrived at the ice cream truck, Amber's friends stormed the truck as well.

"Okay, okay -- ice cream for everyone. Let me go to the car and get some more money. I'll be right back," Vino said. As he pulled the door handle, the car shook; rocks and the ground began to shake. Everything seemed to slow down, a subtle haste even. The ground shifted, followed by an array of colors – red, orange, yellow, and blue -- followed by a violent combustion of metal, heat, and debris; obliterating almost everything and everyone within a half block radius.

When calamity over takes you like a storm, when disaster engulfs you like a cyclone, and anguish and distress overwhelm you. When they cry for help, I will not answer. Though they anxiously search for me, they will not find me. For they hated knowledge and chose not to fear the Lord. They rejected my advice and paid no attention when I corrected them. Therefore, they must eat the bitter fruit of living their own way. Choking on their schemes. For simpletons turn away from me – to death…

Secrets Breed Destruction

Glendale, Arizona
April 29, 2012
11:56 pm

"Why would you call me here. Are you crazy?" Olivia said as she walked out of Ty's hospital room.

"I didn't have much of a choice. I'm not trying to put you in a compromising position. I'm just worried about you," a man answered.

"I'm fine," Olivia replied. "Any word from ***there***?"

"Not much, but he's growing impatient. He's ready to make a move," The man replied.

"Just keep me informed. I have to go. Don't call me again while I'm here," Olivia said, hanging up the phone. She hated her circumstances and the situations that put her at odds with her affection for Ty. She walked back into the room, staring at Ty who showed no sign of life. Mona made arrangements for Ty to be sent home and overseen around the clock by their doctors. If he was to die, Mona wanted him to pass in the confines of his home, not in some hospital.

Olivia sat next to Ty and held his hand. The machines beeped, providing him air and the assurance that he was still alive. "*I wish you were here right now to help me through all the chaos in my life,"* Olivia said as if Ty could hear her. *"Sometimes, I don't even know what I'm doing is even right anymore. I never told you, but I got a nine-year old daughter. Her name is Lauryn. She lives with my mom in Portland."* Olivia valued Ty's friendship. They spent hours talking on the phone when he wasn't in Arizona. Olivia walked out of the room and made a call to someone she did not want to speak with.

"Remember that favor you owe me?" Olivia asked. "Well, I need it now."

The person on the other end waited seconds before answering. "Terrance Writter!" the voice revealed as he hung up.

***

Florence, Italy
May 3, 2012
9:36 am

Mona loved Vino like a son. His tragic departure was a great loss to her. But she knew that in war, there would be casualties determined by providence, leaving us unable to choose who stays and who goes. War is a cause in which blood is the ink used to write the markings on the wall, the wall of vanity.

Mona and Anisa had flown to Florence, Italy to offer their condolences to Vino's family. Although his death was tragic, the lives of his daughters were not just collateral damage. It was senseless. War had no boundaries, but even Mona saw no purpose in harming children. Carlos crossed a line with this cowardly act. Mona saw to it that Vino's ashes were returned to his home. His family was grateful.

While Vino's mother was speaking at his funeral, Mona's thoughts were interrupted when Anisa whispered that Cynthia Davis and her agent were standing at the front gates. Mona and Anisa left the service to speak with Cynthia. "Let's talk away from the service," Mona said as they walked a short distance from the speaker.

When the agent began to search Mona, Anisa jumped between the two of them. "You touch her, I'll put you in one of these graves," Anisa promised.

"Agent Smith, it's alright," Cynthia said. Anisa bumped Agent Smith, allowing Mona to walk in front of the agent. "The Director is pushing hard. He wants you to be brought in. Hell, the Director and President are putting together a Task Force. Somebody has to answer for the bombing that killed the children. You have to disappear."

"Seems like we have a problem," Mona said. "You tell the Director the fun hasn't even begun. And that we take no claim in harming children."

"But Mona, it's a result of your Syndicate feuding with another. They're calling this an act of terrorism. I can't protect you anymore. The F.B.I. is in on this now."

"I have to finish what was started. You do what you think is necessary. I will," Mona replied with nothing short of a promise.

"Why take the chance of losing everything you have?"

"The most prized possessions that anyone can have are family and respect," Mona replied. "Both have been violated. My decision is final."

Cynthia looked at her childhood friend and felt nothing but pity. The girl she once knew was gone. All Cynthia saw now was a stranger. While Mona and Cynthia loved each other, the lines had been drawn a long time ago.

Mona looked at Agent Smith from a distance. "You training rookies again?" Mona joked.

"I like to have my own people. Inside sources are always an advantage. Hopefully, Anisa doesn't kill him before he becomes useful," Cynthia replied. "You don't have to worry about him."

"Who said I was worried?" Mona asked, walking off.

Anisa quickly caught up with Mona. "What do you want me to do?" Anisa asked.

"Let them make the first move. Cynthia's a smart woman. She'll figure something out," replied Mona.

"You know I'm with you, no matter what," Anisa said. "But I think Cynthia's right. Things are about to get bad. The bombing of kids is an issue to be concerned about."

"Blood spills on both sides – those who aren't innocent as well as those who are," Mona explained. "You think when the Pentagon orders bombings that kill hundreds of innocent people they mourn about it? No! This is a war, nothing to be emotionally attached to. My son may die, and I'm guaranteed to not shed a tear because death is synonymous with the culture we live in. I would rather die on the very soil where I spilled blood, than die in chains in some concrete box. My fight is here, not running away from it." Anisa didn't say another word or ask another question. She feared the thought of losing Mona and being left alone. While Anisa was willing to give her own life to protect her, Mona was stubborn. Mona knew Anisa was scared, not of war or death, but the fact that things could change.

***

Chicago, Illinois
May 7, 2012
6:45 pm

"You're quite a story aren't you?" Mona said as she sat across from Yatta.

"We all got a story to tell," Yatta replied as he gave Mona the documents, turning things back to Peter's name.

"How do we proceed now with Peter being dead?" Mona asked. "I'm not too trusting of strangers. Can I trust you?"

"Trust don't have anything to do with being honest," Yatta replied. I treat people how I want to be treated, that simple."

"Did you treat Peter fair by strong arming him for something he helped build?" Mona asked.

"That's different," Yatta answered. "He put me in prison. I should've put him in the ground, but I didn't."

"How would you like to work for me?" Mona asked straight out.

"Doing what?"

"You're a smart man. You know the nature of the business I indulge in," Mona replied.

"You run two companies worth billions of dollars, so why have your hands in anything beneath that?" Yatta asked.

"When you're looking at the capital, it makes a lot of sense. But there's a lot of moving parts that enables a fortune. You can never lose sight of the things that get you ahead. I'm never one to forget those who've sacrificed for the cause," Mona explained.

While she was talking, Yatta found a lot of her words to be noble. She was a woman of principle. "Do you always bring strangers into your organization?" Yatta asked.

Mona laughed. "I probably know more about you than you know about yourself. I don't deal in uncertainty. You don't last long in this world being unsure."

"What about trust?" Yatta asked. "How do you know that you can trust me?"

"You're still alive aren't you?" Mona responded. I don't play well with others that steal from me, but I have my reasons as to why I do things."

"So, what's next with these documents that I have drafted back to a dead man?"

Yatta asked.

"For now, they'll stay in his name until my people make other arrangements. Anisa will contact you at a later time." Mona said as she left Yatta to his thoughts. He had never met a woman like Mona.

***

Reno, Nevada
May 9, 2012
11:00 am

Carlos joined Governor Perez and a congressman for a game of golf. "I never found golf to really be a sport, but who am I to say," Carlos said. Governor Perez seemed irritated by Carlos' remark.

"What brings you to this side of town?" the governor asked.

Carlos and Governor Perez knew each other well. Before Perez became governor, he and Carlos did business together and had a mutual understanding. That was before things went south and the governor cut ties with Carlos. The congressman excused himself, giving Carlos and the governor some privacy. "It's always an honor to walk amongst the privileged," Carlos said as he swung his club, missing the ball completely.

"I know you well enough to know you're here for a reason, not to walk amongst the privileged," the governor said.

"You made arrangements for The Royal Diamond Casino and Resort to be in operation. So, I want you to terminate all of their permits and not to be reinstated," Carlos said.

"You know I can't do that," the governor said. "I can't go against my word. Besides, there has to be a reason to terminate their permits."

"Here's what's going to happen," Carlos said with a stern voice. "You're going to have a talk with Mr. Donovan, a member of the Gambling Commissioners Board, and advise him that you made a mistake allowing them to open. If I have to do things my way, you'll be on the phone with

The President, begging him to deploy the fucking National Guard," Carlos snapped.

"I'll make the call, but after this we are done," the governor said as he quickly left.

Shit is unpleasant, but if you dwell in it too long, you'll get use to it…

"Mona Takes A Trip To Miami."

Chicago, Illinois
May 14, 2012
1:37 pm

Yatta's was preoccupied with what transpired at Peter's house. Someone was going out of their way to keep certain things from resurfacing. Yatta also wondered about Mona's motives. Why would she allow him to be part of a Syndicate larger than anything he could imagine?

"I got a hard time trusting these people," Key said to Yatta while he waited for Anisa to pick him up. He had no idea as to where they were going or what they were going to do.

"If they wanted to harm us, they have the means to do so. But my guard is up, for sure," Yatta replied.

A few minutes passed before a black town car pulled up to escort Yatta to Anisa's location. After a forty-minute drive, Yatta found himself boarding a lavish private jet; the wood-grain finish and gold panels complemented the décor; and the crème and white carpet synchronized with the leather seats.

Anisa was sitting in a seat. "Let's get something straight," Anisa said. "If you think about crossing Mona or bringing her any harm, I will kill you and everyone you love."

"I believe you," Yatta said. "Good thing I don't plan on doing either."

"Good. We got to pay someone a visit. Buckle up," Anisa said, closing her eyes as the plane was set to take off.

***

Los Angeles, California
May 17, 2012
11:43 pm

"Just run the fucking light," Victor yelled at the limo driver. Victor and his friend, Alex Straus, were celebrating their victory – Alex was elected as City Councilman. Now they were traveling in a limo full of Russian hookers and cocaine. "To the new California councilman," Victor yelled as he snorted a line of coke snaked across the woman's breast.

"I couldn't have done it without you. This is our victory," Alex admitted. The limo driver came to a sudden stop, causing Victor to spill his drink and hit the partition.

"Hey moron, you're fired," Victor snapped. "I'm going to make sure you don't drive another day of your life." Tires could be heard sliding as the driver pushed his foot onto the brake pedal. Victor pulled the curtain back and saw two trucks blocking them in.

"What the hell is this?" Victor yelled. Alex was petrified, with no idea what was going on. Victor opened the door and saw silver Lamborghini Gallardo come flying around the corner. When it stopped, Anisa emerged from the driver's seat. She was adorned in a scarlet Dolce Gabanna dress and heels. Victory got back in the limo with a nervous look on his face.

"Is everything alright Victor?" Alex nervously asked.

"Yeah, of course," Victor replied unconvincingly. Anisa got inside the limo and closed the door behind her. Yatta occupied the passenger seat.

"Hello Victor," Anisa said. "You look like you're celebrating something. Did I interrupt anything?"

Victor cleared his throat. "My friend Alex Straus just won the councilman's seat, so we thought we would have a night out."

Anisa really didn't care. "Cynthia Davis paid Mona a surprise visit. So, we want to know how this happened without giving Mona a heads up? After all, you're getting paid well to inform us of these things. Also, we were warned about a possible raid, but not from you."

"I can't predict Cynthia's moves. She's the Assistant Director of the C.I.A. for Christ sakes," Victor replied. "I wouldn't know anything about that until it's declassified and sent to the lower departments."

"You're an intel officer," Anisa said, "so either you're lying or you're just an incompetent idiot."

"Had I known anything about a raid against Mona, I would have rushed to contact her," Victor vented. "But you do have an undercover Agent in your organization. That I do know."

"Keep talking," Anisa said.

"All I know is that she's an Intelligence Officer and her file is sealed. Nobody can identify her but the Director. There's not even an evacuation plan for the mole. This mission is considered a detachable operation, meaning it's off the books and classified," Victor explained.

"You've got two days to find out who this mole is and I don't care what you have to do," Anisa demanded. "Get it done or my next visit won't be so understanding."

"I would have to contact Terrence Writter. He has the address of all black sites and the names of all sleeper agents in the field," Victor said.

"Don't make me come back," Anisa said, turning her attention to Alex. "I'm a huge fan of your work."

"I'm glad I could be of service. I see you know good politics," Alex shot back with a huge smile.

"Actually, I hate everything about politics, especially the politicians," Anisa said as she unholstered her weapon, shot Alex in the head, and unloaded on the Russian hookers.

"He's a councilman!" Victor yelled.

"He was. You have a good day Victor," Anisa said. Yatta got out of the front seat of the limo, and entered the Lamborghini with Anisa as they sped off.

***

Miami, Florida
May 24, 2012
1:16 pm

Mona pulled out of her garage in a white and silver Bugatti Vernon. She had a meeting with an old friend and decided to drive herself, something she rarely did. Although Anisa was at the mansion, Mona insisted on driving alone. Mona blew through traffic, failing to beat a traffic light. She hated being caught at red lights.

"Asil Anom!" Mona said to herself. While Mona stayed with her thoughts, she noticed a black SUV following her. For safety's sake, Mona made a left turn. So did the truck. She pulled the Glock 17 from her center console. When she slowed down, the truck sped up, smashing into the back of her car. Then another truck appeared, hitting the passenger side of the car. Mona was pinned next to a truck with no place to go. The gun fell from her hand. Several men emerged from the trucks, unloading multiple rounds. The bulletproof material that cloaked the vehicle was holding up, but for how long? Pedestrians were ducking, running for cover as the chaos unfolded. Mona knew time was against her. She tried to move but her right arm was broken. She grabbed her gun, crawled into the back seat where the door opened just enough for her to squeeze out.

Boom!

Boom!

Boom!

Boom!

Although Mona unloaded a few shots, she was being bombarded with gunfire.

Boom!

Boom!

She shot back, but the assailants had too much firepower. Mona heard footsteps closing in on her. She then ran to the rear of a truck that covered her. They were still shooting at her. One bullet caught Mona in her shoulder. She fell against the truck and didn't move. While waiting her fate, a Range Rover with three police cruisers pulled up. Anisa jumped out of the truck, firing rapidly as she raced towards Mona. The policemen engaged the other assailants and made a perimeter around the route Anisa had taken. Mona had nearly the entire Miami Police Department under her payroll, so their aid wasn't just an act of due diligence. It was their job. Anisa rolled forward and came up on one knee.

Boc!

Boc!

Boc!

Boc!

She dropped both men who had cornered Mona. Anisa then ran to Mona, helping her off the ground. Seeing that Mona was hurt, made Anisa's blood boil over in anger. Once she pulled Mona into the truck, they sped from the scene.

When it rains, it pours!!!

***

Location Classified
F.B.I. Blacksite
May 29, 2012

"I'm here, where are you?" Agent Kemp said as she continually looked around.

"Right in front of you," Terrance Writter replied, and then hung up.

Kemp approached Terrance and spoke. "You have an open line with other intel officers. You have to cut ties with them or all blacksites and sleeper agents will be compromised," Agent Kemp assured him.

"I think we can hold things together on our end," Terrance said. "We're seasoned Field Agents."

"This isn't Quantico," Agent Kemp said. "Mona isn't someone we can make a mistake with. She will exploit it."

"Thanks for wasting my time. I thought you called because you had some information," Terrance said, walking off.

"Shit!" Agent Kemp mumbled as she left with nothing accomplished.

Peace Between Enemies

Miami, Florida
June 1, 2012
9:15 pm

"You think now is a good time to make that call?" Kema asked Anisa as they drove down the back roads near the Everglades.

"We can handle ourselves, besides it's too soon to call in favors," Anisa said as they drove by a police cruiser parked in a ditch.

"I thought you checked the back roads for cops?" Anisa said as she looked in her rear view mirror.

"I did. He must have just appeared," Kema said. They were enroute to meet someone at the private airstrip half a mile down the road.

Red and blue lights flashed repeatedly, interrupting the darkness of a summer night. Anisa pulled over as the police cruiser followed closely behind. The back roads were isolated and secluded from the busy streets of Miami; mostly open to the Everglades and small planes that landed on private airstrips.

The officer slowly emerged from his cruiser and approached the vehicle. Anisa and Kema were both under the provision of the Russian counsel, making them both diplomatic citizens. The vehicle was also registered to the Embassy and considered diplomatic property, causing Anisa to question the stop.

"Is there a problem officer?" Anisa asked as she lowered the window.

"No, not at all young lady," the officer answered. "Just don't get much company back here, so this is a concerned safety stop." Anisa smiled. Kema remained composed, yet vigilant.

"We're alright officer, just taking this road to the air strip ahead," explained Anisa.

"Well, I see you women are alright, so I'll let you go on your way," the officer said as he stepped back, unholstered his service weapon and fired into the vehicle. The first trajectory grazed Anisa's cheek as she managed to duck the second one. Kema jumped from the car and returned fire. Anisa followed in unison. A series of shots sent the officer running for cover. Kema closed in and fired at the fleeing officer as he managed to fire back. While he made his way to the driver's side of the car, he saw Anisa. But it was too late. She fired a shot that ripped through the officer's clavicle.

"Ah shit," he yelled in excruciating pain. Anisa walked up close as Kema made her way around the car.

"Who do you think he works for?" Kema asked.

"The Cuadras Cartel, definitely," Anisa said, firing a bullet into his skull.

"Are you okay?" Kema asked.

"Yeah, it's just a graze wound," Anisa answered. "Let's get out of here. I'm sure someone heard the shots.

***

Miami, Florida
June 6, 2012
1:16 pm

Mona sat across the table from Carlos. Her arm was in a sling, looking as if she had been in a battle. Both leaders brought enough armed men that could cause a catastrophic chain of reactions. Mona agreed to meet with

Carlos on neutral grounds and talk. She only wanted to meet him out of curiosity, not peace talks. She wanted to taunt him for the times he pursued her.

"This is a war that neither of us can win without losing everything," Carlos said. "You're a woman of strong conviction and undeterred pride. I got it. But we've lost enough people. My son Vinny failed to respect the code and the structural building blocks used to climb the ladder of civility." Mona concentrated as Carlos spoke. "I'm not here to mend any bridges, but to call a peace treaty to allow us the time to mourn," Carlos explained.

"You made an attempt on my life, nearly killed my son, blew up one of my associates, and killed two innocent kids. Now you want to call for a peace treaty?" Mona argued.

"Do you want me to run down the list of people who died on my side?" Carlos asked. "You took innocent people from me as well, so let's not make my acts seem as if they're undisciplined."

"War is inevitable when two groups are seeking the same thing," Mona said. "In this business, blood is used to sign the contracts we endorse. We were once friends, now on divided sides of placidity. I'm more than willing to put everything on the line right now, and die if that's what it comes to. So is everybody behind me. How far are you willing to go, because I'm willing to go all the way," Mona challenged.

"That attempt on your life was only a message," Carlos said. "I could have reached further…"

"That's what separates the two of us. When I reach out, I touch what's meant to be touched. Failure has never been an option," Mona interjected.

"You know why most people fear? Because it keeps them balanced. When one fails to fear, it makes them vulnerable. Fear makes you more focused and alert. That's what you lack," Carlos said as he pulled a weapon from one of his men's holster. Mona's people reacted and drew theirs. Mona held her hand up, ordering her people to lower their weapons. Carlos took the magazine out and removed a slug. Mona did the same.

"In our culture, once you're considered a made man amongst the Italians, no one could break that stature of nobility. You become untouchable," Carlos said as he tossed Mona the slug. Mona did the same.

"I never understood that code but I do respect being loyal to my word. The only thing I can say is that I promise nothing but a grave for your son Vinny," Mona said. Carlos whispered something to one of his men who left, reappearing with a cooler in hand. Carlos sat the cooler on the table and pushed it to Mona. She opened it and found a frozen head – it was Vinny's.

"That's the head of my only son," Carlos replied. Mona gave the cooler to Anisa. Both leaders shook hands and the peace treaty was on. Before Carlos left, he looked Mona in the eyes and spoke. "el Padre que correcta los errors de su hijo, es un Padre quien Jale." With that, he walked off.

"What does that mean?" Anisa asked Mona

"A Father who corrects his son's mistakes is a Father worth being.

***

Atlantic Air Way
Private Jet
June 10, 2012
2:47 pm

Anisa's phone rang. It was Victor. "I gave you two days, tell me why I shouldn't kill you?" Anisa threatened.

"I had a lot of trouble just getting a name and picture of the agent that's within your organization. She's being well protected. I had to call in some favors just to access her orientation file from the service. Her name is Agent Kemp but her C.I. name is being withheld. I'm sending you a picture of her right now!" Victor said, moments later the photo appeared. Anisa was stunned. It was a picture of Olivia, Ty's personal assistant.

"We have a problem!" Anisa said, telling the pilot to turn the jet around and head for Arizona.

***

Chicago, Illinois
June 10, 2012
3:00 pm

Keyanna was a friend that Key held close to her heart; a good listener who provided the balance she needed to maintain her sanity. Key sometimes shared both the illegal and personal things she refused to share with others. When Key asked for advice, Keyanna told her what needed to be done.

Judge Posner slid into his car, turned the ignition key, and was puzzled by why it wouldn't start. He had recently taken it to the garage for a tune up. "What the hell is going on," the Judge thought as he stepped from the car. He lifted the hood and noticed that the battery cables had been disconnected. Key came from nowhere, slamming the hood that caused the Judge to fall to the ground. Key squatted and grabbed a hand full of his hair.

"You was paid a visit not too long ago by a man," Key asked. "What did you tell him?"

"What are you talking about?"

Key replied by slamming his head against the car. "I'm going to ask you one more time. And if it's not the answer I'm looking for, then I will shoot you right here."

"I had to save my wife," the Judge said. "She was going to die. So, I told him what I knew."

"Did you tell him about the girl?" Key asked.

"There wasn't much to tell. I just told him Peter was protecting some girl," Judge Posner admitted.

"Do you know who I am?" Key asked.

The Judge took a long took. "Should I know who you are?"

"Not really!" Key replied, shooting Posner in the head.

Death happens when life stops and secrets fail to threaten the truth. So, lies can be necessary…

A Mole In The Syndicate

Glendale, Arizona
June 11, 2012
2:16 am

While Anisa never suspected Olivia of being a mole, she never trusted her. She believed Olivia held a secret that needed to be revealed. Anisa had been watching Ty's mansion for hours, hoping to find Ty and Olivia. It was time to take a closer look. She unlocked the door and walked inside. Her men stood guard, listening to police scanners in case she radioed for backup. The house looked to be abandoned. Ty's hospital equipment was gone. Anisa pulled out her phone and called Mona. "Olivia is gone. So is Ty."

***

Langley, Virginia
June 19, 2012
1:10 pm

Cynthia Davis left her office after being briefed about a possible raid against Mona.

Cynthia knew that things were about to go from bad to worse. While they were close during their childhood days, Cynthia believed that Mona had changed over the years. At times, Cynthia felt like she was Mona's slave, a pawn in her game of chess, and that she needed to pick a side. Her only solution was to capture Mona and lock her away. Even so, Mona would probably find out the responsible party and retaliate. Perhaps Mona should be killed, putting an end to her reign.

Mona told Cynthia that Olivia was the undercover agent within their organization. Cynthia was surprised that Mona had never suspected Olivia to be a mole. While Mona knew at that moment that Cynthia had chosen her side, Mona would deal with her later. She needed Cynthia to find Ty.

***

Chicago, Illinois
June 21, 2012
6:27 pm

"What happened that day, the day you got locked up?" Capone asked Yatta.

"I lived it long enough," Yatta said. "What's the use of talking about it? I cleared my mind a long time ago. What's done is done. No matter how much I think about it or talk about it, I can't get the years back that I spent in the cage."

"When you left, shit got bad," Capone said. "Everything fell apart. But Deno and me kept each other straight. You already know why a nigga wasn't getting at you while you was in that box. We couldn't see you like that, and the circumstances we dealt with everyday."

"Good thing we ain't got to struggle no more. As long as we're on board with Mona, I think shit going to be better than expected," Yatta added.

"She's unpredictable and that can be dangerous," Capone replied. Yatta had never dealt with anyone who played the game at this height. Mona had the means to do whatsoever she pleased. But for some reason, his gut told him to trust her.

"We couldn't do what I planned for the documents we got from Peter because Mona's two companies are financed by The Sheridan Corporation," Yatta said.

"Now it all make sense," Capone said. "The Sheridan Corporation and The Sheridan Syndicate. She was using Peter and his political ties." Capone had put two and two together.

"I don't know who killed Peter, but the timing was too coincidental. I think somebody is going out of their way to keep something from resurfacing," Yatta said.

"Yo, that bitch Anisa, she fine ass, hell, she just need some anger management," Capone said switching the subject.

"Any broad that's licensed to carry a gun, I don't want any relations with," Yatta shot back as he headed to the front door. "I got to make a run. I'll catch you later."

***

Langley, Virginia
June 23, 2012
1:10 pm

Terrence Writter was jogging the outside trails when he ran upon an attractive woman on the ground holding her ankle. He quickly stopped. "Are you alright?" Terrence asked.

"I think it's sprained, rolled it pretty bad."

"You tried putting some weight on it?" Terrance asked as he grabbed at her ankle. The woman winced in pain. "Well, the good thing is, it's not broken. Here, let me help you up. You have a car anywhere or do you live nearby?" he asked.

"My car is parked on the bottom of the runway," the woman said. Terrence helped the woman to her car where she took the bag from her shoulder and handed it to Terrence. "Can you put this in the trunk for me?" she asked politely. As Terrance opened the trunk Kema tasered him, then pushed him into the trunk. She knew Terrence would fall for *the injured pretty woman in the park act.*

The ride seemed to last forever. When the car finally stopped, Terrence braced himself for what Kema might do. Mona and Anisa stood, waiting on Kema to open the trunk. Although Terrence had never met Mona, he was aware of her reputation.

"Do you know who I am Mr. Writter?" Mona asked.

"Do you know you just assaulted and kidnapped a Federal Agent?" He shot back.

Mona smiled, then shared her demands. "I want to know the whereabouts of Agent Kemp." Terrence was surprised by the information she possessed, and how he worked for the agency, struggling to get information on Kemp.

"Before you speak, think to yourself. How did I find you and manage to extract you from within the confines of a C.I.A. compound? I'm not here to pull your teeth for information. I ask the questions and you answer them. Simple," Mona explained.

"I don—"

Psst!

Anisa's silencer smoked, waiting to unleash another bullet. Terrence growled in agony, cursing a rant of assaults that neither of the women took serious. Anisa then shoved her gun into Terrence's groin. "The next time it won't be a knee cap. It'll be in a place much worse," Anisa promised. Terrence believed her.

“Where is the black site used to hide Agent Kemp?” Mona asked.

“El Paso, Texas,” Terrence said. “She’s in Texas.”

“How do I know you’re not lying?” Mona replied.

“I swear it. She’s there,” Terrence answered.

Mona got into the car with Anisa and sped off. Terrence didn’t see Kema as he limped towards the main street for help. He pulled out his cell phone and called Cynthia Davis. “I just got fucking shot and kidnapped by Mona. You have to warn Agent Ke---“

Psst!

Psst!

Psst!

Kema shot Terrence dead, picked up his phone from the ground. “Let me guess – Cynthia Davis?” Kema spoke.

“Who is this?” Cynthia replied.

“Someone you’ll see soon,” Kema said, throwing the phone into the lake.

Ain’t much of a balance that you’ll find when you dwell amongst chaos and pandemonium. You live and die in the world you create. Rather by compromise or disdain. You can follow all the rules and find the path to peace, but it’ll all be in vain, because you’re bound to find danger at your doorstep – sooner or later…

A Game Of Blackjacks

Reno, Nevada
June 27, 2012
2:00 pm

Governor Perez walked inside The Royal Diamond Casino and Resort that was officially shut down and decommissioned from all services open to the public. "Have a seat Governor," Sky said as The Governor walked into his office.

"I don't have much time son. I only agreed to meet out of respect for Vino Arturo," The Governor said. To be truthful, Governor Perez knew nothing about Vino's personal matters. But Governor Perez knew that Sky was one of Mona's sons, and that all of her people were not to be taken lightly.

"You play blackjack Governor?" Sky asked.

"I used to, but that was many years ago. I haven't played for quite some time son," the Governor answered.

"I like blackjack. Mainly, because it's a game governed by a set of rules. For instance, if you go over twenty-one, you lose," Sky said, looking at the deck of cards in his hand. "Let's go down to the gambling tables and play a few hands," Sky said as he stood up.

"I'm a bit pressed for time. Maybe at a later time," the Governor said.

"I insist," Sky demanded. The Governor followed Sky to the gambling tables where a young lady sat. But she wasn't there to deal cards. "This is Kema, an associate of mine," Sky said, removing his suit jacket, rolling up his sleeves. Sky picked up the deck and dealt a card to the Governor.

"The permits and codes needed to operate this business have been terminated. So, I looked deeper into this concerning matter – stay or hit?" Sky asked the Governor as he picked up his cards.

"Hit," the Governor said. "I had no idea what happened until I got the notice on my desk. In fact, I was wondering, why would Mr. Donovan do such a thing?

"The Gambling Commissioner acted on his own recognizance. I had absolutely nothing to do with this," the Governor explained.

"I take you as an honorable man, Governor. Am I correct?" Sky asked.

"Of course. I think that's the best way to be," the Governor added.

"Would you lie to me, Governor?" Sky asked, looking into the Governor's eyes.

"Son, my word and reputation are all I got."

"I believe you Governor," Sky said as he dealt more cards.

"Bust, you lose!" Sky said. The Governor's cards exceeded twenty-one. "I have a surprise for you." Kema returned with Mr. Donovan who was blindfolded and bound by his hands. The Governor was shocked.

"What is the meaning of this?" The Governor's voice rose.

"You said Mr. Donovan was the one who shut down my business, and you're an honorable man, I believe you. Since we were both baffled as to why he shut us down, maybe he can explain," Sky explained.

"Mr. Donovan had nothing to do with shutting you down. It was me," the Governor admitted. "Carlos told me I had no choice but to shut you down or he would do so by other means."

"Mr. Governor, you lied to me and broke the trust that I thought we had," Sky said, turning his attention to Mr. Donovan. "How long would it take to fix the permits and undo what our Governor did?"

"Twenty-four hours," Mr. Donovan said.

"Kema, kill the Governor and make certain our Gambling Commissioner knows the severity of this situation," Sky said as he put his suit jacket on. Kema blew the Governor's brains out, then turned to the Gambling Commissioner.

"If it was up to me, I would kill you too, but I'm not here to make that decision. So, if I have to come looking for you, you're not going to like it," Kema said. Mr. Donovan understood.

All gambles come at a risk, so only gamble if you're willing to lose it all…

***

Chicago, Illinois
July 1, 2012
9:16 am

Anisa had made arrangements for Yatta to be picked up by one of their drivers. When Yatta arrived at the private airstrip, he found Anisa waiting on the jet. She passed him a glass of expensive champagne. He sat across from her, admiring her beauty.

"I see you guys take business serious and in luxury," Yatta said as he looked around the private jet.

"Of course we take business serious. The luxury is just an accommodation for our work ethic. Buckle up, we're heading to Miami."

***

El Paso, Texas
July 1, 2012
11:30 am

Agent Kemp was hiding in a black site located in El Paso, Texas. She left Ty's mansion in Arizona hours before Mona and Kema arrived. She took Ty with her, but didn't know why. Although Ty was in stable condition, he appeared lifeless. Agent Kemp notified her superiors, telling them that she had Ty and was waiting for further instructions.

Mona had an abundance of resources and wasn't someone Agent Kemp wanted after her. Kemp called Cynthia Davis, the only person she could trust. "I need your help," Kemp said the moment Cynthia answered.

"Why haven't you followed protocol?" Cynthia asked. "You're expected to report back for debriefing."

"I can't right now. I'll explain later, just not over the phone. I need a safe house, one that is off the books."

"Sure, how is Ty doing?" Cynthia asked.

"He's stable for now. But he needs to be in a more secure environment."

"Agent Kemp, you shouldn't have contacted Terrence…"

"How do you know about Terrence Writter," Kemp asked with a nervous tone to her voice. "Nobody but the Director knew that Terrence and I had made contact."

"You are in well over your head," Cynthia warned. "If I was you, I would have left Ty there and let Mona take him. You will die otherwise."

"Oh my God. You're working for her. You're working for Mona?" Agent Kemp was shocked by the revelation.

"She knows you're in El Paso," Cynthia stated. "You can thank Terrence for that. She's coming for you an…" Agent Kemp hung up, packed her things, strapped her vest on, and checked her weapon. She was thankful that most of Ty's equipment was transportable. Kemp was moving as fast as she could. Mona was coming.

***

Miami, Florida
July 1, 2012
12:45 am

"Asil anom!" Mona said to herself while sitting at her desk studying a map, the same map she'd been examining for the past four years.

While deep in her thoughts, Anisa walked in. "Yatta's downstairs. Kema should be landing in El Paso any minute," Anisa said.

"Good, you can send him up," Mona replied. Mona rolled up the map when Yatta walked into her office. A woman had never intimidated Yatta, but Mona intrigued him in ways he never experienced. As Yatta took his seat, Anisa stood near the door, offering her continuous protection.

"Have you ever heard of the word *Penumbra*?" Mona asked as she sat on the edge of her desk

"Can't say I have," Yatta admitted.

"*Penumbra* is a partial shadow, a fraction of a shadow. We're all *penumbras* to each other, but when we're together, that's what makes us one solid shadow. Now back to our previous conversation. I'm willing to put $10 million into your account. All I ask is that you stay on call, and don't speak of things that concerns the welfare of those within the organization."

"I still don't get it. Why take a chance on bringing a stranger into your organization?" Yatta had no idea as to why Mona wanted him. "It seems too good to be true, and when that happens, it is."

Mona leaned forward, speaking with strong certainty. "You know too much about my business to not be part of it." Yatta understood her logic, but there's something else – something she's not telling him. Mona was very shrewd, a vindictive and sometimes unpredictable leader. Yatta knew that for whatever reason Mona wanted him around, she wasn't going to reveal it at this time.

***

El Paso, Texas
Black Site
July 1, 2012
1:00 pm

Kema's men breached the safe house, making certain it was clear. She walked through, looking for any sign that Ty had been there. Kema then called Mona. "She's not here. Ty's not either." Mona wasn't surprised, knowing that Agent Kemp was smart enough to keep moving. "What should I do now?" Kema asked.

"Come home," Mona replied. "She'll make a mistake and we'll be there to catch it." Kema hated the fact that she couldn't bring Ty home. But eventually Agent Kemp would slip up and Kema would put a bullet in her head.

"Let's go!" Kema told the men as she put her shades on and walked out of the house.

Agent On The Run

Neuquen, Argentina
July 2, 2012
3:59 pm

Carlos was meeting with Shawn Fertz, an Executive Bank Manager who was handling a few of his offshore accounts. "You've come a long distance. This must be important," Shawn said to Carlos as they shook hands and took their seats.

"Some things require a face to face meeting," Carlos replied. "I prefer handling business this way. Now, I paid you a large amount of money for something in return. You promised to launder the capital from my business based in Mexico. I received an updated audit from my lawyer, and it's short by a lot."

"Carlos, we had certain arrangements but there was a problem. There was too much capital to clean on one run. Our bank has a reputation for being clean cut. If your accounts go from two hundred million to a half a billion dollars in a matter of months, that waves a red flag."

"So, you're basically holding my money until you think it's safe to deposit it?" Carlos asked.

"Actually, it's invested," Shawn replied. "You're guaranteed to get it back. It's the best way I could make it legit."

Carlos laughed with a bit of sarcasm. "You have a week to transfer my money or, let's just say you wouldn't want to piss me off," Carlos said as he stood and left the bank.

***

Minneapolis, Minnesota
July 4, 2012
10:00 am

"For a minute, I thought no one would move into that house," Tasha said to her new neighbor.

"My father owns it. He hasn't been here in a number of years. So, I decided to use it for a while. I'm Brittany – Brittany White," Agent Kemp said as she greeted her neighbor. While Kemp was truthful about the house belonging to her father, her real name was not Brittany White.

"Well, I'll let you finish getting things put together," Tasha said. "Talk to you later."

Agent Kemp heard that Terrence Writter had been killed, and that Cynthia Davis pushed hard for her to turn herself in. But Kemp chose to evade everyone until she knew whom to trust. For all she knew, the Director was probably on Mona's payroll.

Agent Kemp thought about Ty, wondering if he would understand why she was an agent. While he might feel betrayed, perhaps her years of service would prove her loyalty. But she couldn't worry about that now. The agency and Ty's vindictive mother were after her. While Kemp worked at doing her job, she had fallen in love with her mark -- Ty.

The moment you find something worth fighting for, then you'll discover what it means to sacrifice…

***

Juneau, Canada
July 11, 2012
8:17 am

Mona called everyone in for a meeting to discuss Ty's situation and other business related issues. Yatta sat at the round table in amazement. The entire estate was massive and the conference room was the size of a ballroom. Yatta had never witnessed an operation this large. All of the hustling wasn't about drug peddling. It was just a stepping-stone.

"Everyone sitting at this table is family, willing to die for one another. All of the other things are just part of the lifestyle. The cars, money, homes, you name it we have it. My only rule is loyalty," Mona explained to Yatta. "Welcome to the table. Let's get down to business."

"Ty was kidnapped by an Agent that infiltrated our Syndicate. Our priority is getting him back, and Agent Kemp if possible. We need to know what she told her superiors, if she told them anything at all," Mona explained.

"What about calling the tracker, Mongo?" Anisa asked. Mongo specialized in tracking people and extracting information. He was from Africa and good at his job.

"You can bring Mongo in, but our pursuit will continue as well," Mona replied. "As far as the Sheridan Corporation, I have a management team running things and securing the accounts. We have the federal government breathing down our necks. We must remain alert at all times."

"Although The Cuadras Cartel and their emissaries, The Mendoza Cartel, agreed to a peace treaty, keep your men on standby," Mona instructed. "If they rub our shoulders slightly, you let your men off the leash." The meeting continued until Mona dismissed everyone but Yatta. She wanted to speak privately to him.

"Your question of trust is a lingering thought. All I can say is to trust my judgment. Some things are best left unanswered. I didn't come this far by making bad decisions," Mona explained.

"Peter said something similar to me. I think I beg to differ," Yatta replied. "Unanswered questions are just that, unanswered questions, no clarity."

"You have the slightest idea as to what you're in for?" Mona asked.

"Is that good or bad?" Yatta wanted to know.

"Let's just say it's not boring. Good things can be bad, but bad can bring out the good in most people, not all," Mona said with a smile on her face.

Yatta liked her, knowing that she could be trusted. But then again, you never know. Mona was full of surprises. "You know how I became so successful?" Mona asked.

"Shoot!" Yatta replied as he listened.

"I never had any respect for money nor those who valued it," Mona answered. "Instead, I aimed to acquire control of capital, not be controlled by it." While Yatta had never looked at it like this, it all made sense.

Perception is everything, but illusions aren't. So, don't be deceived by anything, especially by something that'll expire…

Showdown In New York City

New York, New York
July 17, 2012
2:40 pm

Things had been awkward between Sky and Kema, especially when they were alone. They managed to keep their fling away from Mona. Kema was required to accompany Sky on all of his business trips. That was her job. Sky and Kema were flying to New York where Sky owned a brokerage firm that bought stocks, bonds, and exchanged goods of high value. Kema on the other hand, loved New York for the fashion and other things women found accommodating.

Mona was to attend a meeting for the board of directors that controlled Ty's company. Sky offered to cover the meeting while in New York. Sky was on the phone when the driver made the wrong turn. "You made a wrong turn – turn around and take Fifth Avenue," Sky shouted to the driver. There was a cop directing traffic, making things more complicated. The officer directed the driver to turn down an alley, making Kema suspicious. Although there was a peace treaty with The Cuadras Cartel, she knew the Cartel had many of the New York policemen on their payroll. Carlos couldn't be trusted and Kema didn't trust the peace treaty.

"Stop the car," Kema told the driver. He obliged. Something wasn't right and Kema knew it.

"What's up?" Sky asked.

"Something isn't right," Kema said, pulling the weapons from her shoulder holsters. "Driver, do you have a weapon?" Kema asked.

"Anisa told me to never travel without one," the driver said, removing a gun from the center console.

"Sky, take this and get down." Kema gave him one of her guns as she saw two motorcycles through the rearview mirrors. The motorcycles sped up, opening fire that shattered the back window. Kema opened her door, firing back. The driver followed in unison. The motorcycles stopped and the men jumped off. Kema ran towards one, firing with all intentions to kill. The driver covered her, moving forward as well. Sky had moved to the driver's seat where he reversed the truck and stopped. Kema ducked behind a dumpster and waited. One of the gunmen emerged. Kema shot twice. Both bullets opened his skull as he hit the ground with a thud. Kema ran to the truck, calling for the driver to join them. He turned toward the truck and ran. One bullet ripped through his torso, another caught him in the neck. As Sky pushed hard on the gas, he collided with a van, causing Kema to nearly fly out of the window.

As Kema gathered herself, more men pulled up in a van. "We've got to move," Kema said, pulling Sky out of the truck. Shots were being fired as Kema returned fire and ducked for cover. "I'm going to cover you. Run toward that court-way building on the other side of the alley," Kema said while reloading her weapon.

"I'm not leaving you," Sky said.

"Sky, you better get the fuck…" A slug ripped through her shoulder. Sky fired multiple shots at the assailant. Police cars arrived on the scene, opening fire. Helicopters hovered above the chaos, reporting what was happening. Kema clenched her fist and jaw muscles, fighting off the horrific pain. Sky stood, shooting ferociously. The gunmen were in a shootout with the NYPD. Sky used that as an advantage, pulling Kema to her feet and moving toward the court-way building.

"I got you," Sky told her as they ran. When they made it inside the building, Sky sat her against the wall, ripping off his suit jacket. "I've got to stop the bleeding. This is going to hurt but I have to do it."

"Just do it!" Kema replied, bracing herself for what was to come. Sky tied her wound tightly. Kema winced in agony. She looked out through the window port, watching police cars and patrol officers surround the building.

"Put your weapons down and come out with your hands up," one of the officers yelled through the bullhorn.

"We can't escape this, at least not both of us," Kema said.

"You tripping right now. We're going to make them do their job and come get us both!" Sky replied. Sky hugged Kema and kissed her lips. "Let's fight them together," Sky suggested. Kema looked into his eyes. "I'm sorry," she said, pushing Sky down the stairs that led to the basement. She then ran out the double doors, firing at the platoon of policemen.

Sky quickly gathered his footing, trying to run up the stairs. A hail of bullets forced him back into the basement. There was no way that Kema could have survived. Sky looked around the basement, feeling a cool breeze brush against his body. The breeze came from a cellar door leading out of the basement. He entered the cellar and saw a series of tunnels. Sky didn't care where the tunnels led; wanting to escape the chaos that had transpired. He felt light headed, blurred vision, and his side was wet with blood. His knees buckled, falling to the ground.

Where there's hell, there's fury. Destruction is only the aftermath of someone's wrath…

***

Minneapolis, Minnesota
July 18, 2012
11:45 am

Yatta found some time to spend with Tasha and Lil J, but unfortunately Lil J was away at his grandmother's house. Tasha held things down at home while Yatta kept grounded on the streets. "You look like you're not getting much sleep," Tasha said as she looked into his eyes.

"I ain't got much time to sleep."

"Boy, who ain't got time to sleep?" Tasha asked. "You sound crazy. Yo ass ain't going to be satisfied until you pass out." While they were talking, the doorbell rang. Tasha went to answer it. It was Brittany.

"Yatta, this is Brittany from next door. She just moved in across the street."

Yatta greeted her with a warm welcoming. Brittany was attractive, and Yatta found it strange that she didn't wear a wedding ring. "So where are you from?" Yatta asked.

"I'm from right here in Minnesota, not so much Minneapolis. I grew up in St. Paul," Brittany said.

"So, it's just you in that big house?" Yatta asked.

"No, my brother is with me," Brittany said. "He's kind of sick. I'm his caretaker."

"You don't have to answer any of his questions. Don't mind him," Tasha said.

"I'm just trying to make sure home girl cool. You ain't got no bodies hidden in your basement do you?" Yatta joked.

"Maybe. I haven't checked lately," she replied playfully.

"I'm going to let you ladies do y'all thing. I got to take me a power nap," Yatta said, heading upstairs. He had no idea that Brittany was really Agent Kemp, and that Ty was next door.

***

Miami, Florida
July 18, 2012
1:30 pm

> *Yesterday at approximately 3:00 pm, there was a brazen shootout between two groups of people that haven't been identified at this time. When policemen arrived on the scene, a shootout between them and the assailants ensued. As a result of the chaos, four officers were killed and six of the assailants. There…" That was all Mona needed to hear as she turned off the T.V. She was livid and consumed in worry. There was nothing definitive as to whether Kema and Sky were dead or in custody.*

"I've got people looking into this as we speak," Anisa said. Mona knew Anisa was filled with worry, but pride concealed their concerns.

"You go find out if the Cuadras is behind this. Let's get some answers and deal with matters of action later," Mona instructed her. Mona had allowed Carlos to deceive her and bring harm to her family. While she always played by the rules, Carlos knew that and preyed upon it.

"Where are you?" Mona asked.

"I'm in the air. Should land in a few hours," Mongo answered. Mona felt as if she wasn't in control, an unfamiliar feeling for her. She was making plans for something monumental. Mona played with her thoughts. Her gut feeling told her that this wasn't Carlos. Although they were enemies, Carlos was a man of his word. Still, nothing else made sense. It had to be him. Who else had the audacity to attack her family?

Kings govern their kingdoms with control and rules. But when they lose control and there's no rules to govern the people, then what's the use of a king?…

Thirst For Revenge

Sky woke up disoriented and drowsy. He tried to sit up, but was too weak. He noticed that he had an I.V. in his arm and bandages on his rib cage. Sky managed to swing his feet to the side of the bed as he tried to stand. He fell to the floor.

"The floor isn't as comfortable as the bed," a woman's voice announced. Sky looked up and saw a beautiful young lady. Even in such a confusing state of mind, her beauty could not go unnoticed.

"Where am I?" Sky asked in almost a whisper as his throat felt sore and dry.

"I found you passed out in the middle of the street. You were bleeding badly. Good thing I'm a nurse and have some compassion. You were shot twice."

"Who, who are you?" Sky asked as he sat against the wall.

"My name is Marcella – Marcella Sanchez. You came from under the tunnel passages that run under the court-way buildings. You might want to lay low for a while. The cops have a massive manhunt for you. You guys caused a lot of commotion." As she was talking it hit him – Kema!

"The girl I was with, what happened to her?" Sky asked.

"She was killed. I'm sorry," Marcella said.

"I need to use a phone," Sky said. Marcella gave Sky her phone. The Cuadras were behind this hit and Sky wouldn't stop retaliating until Carlos was dead. The war was back on, for sure! Sky had a long conversation with Mona as they spoke in a language only they knew. Mona was relieved to hear his voice, but sadden by the news of Kema's demise. Now she had to break the news to Anisa. When Sky ended the call, he turned his attention back to Marcella.

"Why did you help me?" he asked.

"Because you needed help. I'm pretty sure if I had a shootout with the cops, you would help me," Marcella replied with a bit of humor.

"You must be somebody important?" She asked more so than stated.

"Not at all," Sky replied flatly.

"Well, I have to get back to work. Make yourself at home. I usually don't allow strangers in my home, but I guess I can make an exception. Besides, judging from your expensive Armani suit, the shoes and Rolex, you're use to the finer things in life," Marcella said, leaving Sky to his thoughts. His head continued to throb until he drifted off.

***

Orlando, Florida
July 24, 2012
10:50 pm

Anisa rode in the back seat of the Denali with an assault rifle across her lap. Mona had told her that Kema was dead. Anisa boiled in anger as hatred consumed her thoughts. Instead of tears falling from her eyes, she cried for vengeance and retribution. Her wrath would be felt in both this life and the next.

Carlos owned a small cigar lounge used as a front to store his cleaned bills. When they made it to the location, the streets were empty; the cigar lounge was packed with men that worked or had ties to The Cuadras Cartel. As Anisa approached the front door, it was locked. She stepped back and fired into the door.

"Kick it in!" she ordered. The door flew open as her men stormed the establishment, followed by a brief gunfight. Anisa entered the place, stepping over the dead bodies that blocked the doorway. She made her way to a couple of men who were smoking cigars and unfazed by the dead bodies. Anisa passed her rifle to one of her men and took a seat at the table.

"Why am I here?" Anisa asked both men, Raul and Paul Mendoza. Both men were high officials in The Mendoza Cartel and emissaries to the Cuadras Cartel.

"You like cigars? After all, it is a cigar lounge," Paul said, blowing a puff of smoke in Anisa's face.

"We've got somewhere to be, so let's get on with it. We're both made men. You can't touch us," Raul said with confidence. Anisa smiled, then without hesitation put a bullet in Raul's skull. She then rose from her seat and pressed her gun to the back of Paul's neck.

"My sister was killed in New York. I want to know where to find Carlos?" Anisa demanded.

"I don't know what you're talking about. As for Carlos, I never heard the name before," Paul replied. Anisa stood back and pulled the trigger. Paul's head hit the table. Anisa shot him again, just because.

The Russian General

Moscow, Russia
July 29, 2012
11:00 am

Finch Shultz was a high-ranking government official within the Russian Military. He controlled the S.A.S. and the elite K.G.B. before his reign in the military some twenty years ago. Finch had a feud with the Russian Syndicate, leaving things too dangerous for his family. The Russian Syndicate targeted his family, eventually killing his wife.

Mona had ties to the Russian Syndicate through her business ventures. But when Mona caught wind that the Syndicate was planning to kill Finch's daughters, she gave him a heads up. Although she didn't know him, Mona was a mother and that resonated with her more than anything else.

Mona had brought Liam Shultz, brother of Finch Shultz, into her rising empire. While Liam aided Finch in the war against The Russian Syndicate, Mona agreed to take Finch's daughters, Anisa and Kema, who were children at the time. She taught them to be Penumbras, each a partial shadow joining together to become a complete shadow. They had been predominantly raised in the United States with frequent visits to Russia.

Finch felt it best for his daughters to remain with Mona. His military career would only cause him to neglect their attention. But Finch allowed his daughters to train with the K.G.B Forces and learn how to read coded epistles. He didn't want this type of life for his daughters, but it chose them. So he provided them with the tools necessary to survive.

A Russian Prime Minister named Viktor recruited Finch. Because of Finch's understanding of the Russian underworld, he was soon promoted to General and Mission Commander.

Years later, Anisa now watched her little sister, Kema, lowered into a Russian grave. Mona wanted Kema to be buried in her native land. Anisa had never experienced this level of rage, even when she watched her mother being raped and killed. Other than her father, Kema was the last blood family Anisa had. Sky wanted to attend the funeral, but Mona advised him to remain out of sight. She was waiting for her contacts to check any surveillance that would put Sky at risk.

Mona and Finch talked in a whisper. "Do you know who's responsible for this?" Finch inquired.

"Carlos," Mona said. "This was a cowardly act and I will make sure he gets put under my feet."

"How is she doing?" Finch asked as he looked at Anisa from a distance.

"She's disconnected from the world right now; needs time to grieve. She's your child, she's strong."

"Anisa scares me," Finch admitted.

"There's an Agent Kemp who has my son, Ty. I need to know if any of your spies in the states can locate her," Mona asked.

"Will do. I have to get going. You take care of yourself," Finch said as he left the funeral.

"Sky Makes A Friend."

New York, New York
August 1, 2012
8:16 pm

Sky and Marcella had grown close in a short amount of time. She found Sky to be entertaining, and since she did not leave him to die or turned over to the authorities, Sky trusted her. Her freedom was at risk to save his.

Sky and Marcella spent the night watching the Starz hit "*Power*" and eating junk food. Sky couldn't recall the last time he had a night like this. It was better than vacationing in the finest places that money could buy.

"Do you ever wish you could change a few things from your past, besides the obvious?" Marcella asked.

"I never gave that any thought. The world I live in, you have no time to deal in the what ifs." Sky answered as he thought about Ty, wondering what he was going through.

"I have family back in Colombia," Marcella said. "My father is from Mexico, so the mixture of both cultures exposed me to a lot of things."

"I see you're doing well for yourself," Sky complimented as he looked around her apartment.

"I came to the United States to get away from my mother and her bullshit. Once I graduated from nursing school, I took my residency at the hospital here in New York City. Now I call this place home," Marcella said with a smile.

Sky admired her ambition. But for Sky, life had a different plan. "What's your mother like?" Marcella inquired.

"Not the average mother," Sky said. "She's focused, persistent, and I'll leave it at that." It was obvious that there was more to the mystery, but Marcella didn't push it.

"My mother's name is Soria – Soria Sanchez. She runs the Cartels based out of Colombia." Sky was stunned. Soria was their drug supplier and Mona's good friend.

"Your mother's name is Soria Sanchez?" Sky asked again.

"What, you know her?" Marcella asked quizzically.

"Nawl, just a beautiful name." They talked for hours and before they knew it, sleep consumed them.

***

Greatfalls, Montana
August 4, 2012
8:49 am

Cynthia Davis parked in front of her cabin nestled in the remote mountains of Greatfalls, Montana. Cynthia enjoyed the seclusion from civilization; a place to clear her head, discover the answers to a mess she had created.

Agent Smith accompanied her. "We'll figure this out together," the Agent said. Cynthia had handpicked Agent Smith fresh out of training.

"I hope so," Cynthia replied as they carried luggage to the porch. "I think I want to stay here forever. It's so peaceful and quiet."

When they started to open the cabin door, it was unlocked. Agent Smith stopped Cynthia from walking in. "Wait, let me check it out."

"I'm pretty sure it's nothing. No one comes up here. I probably left it unlocked," Cynthia said before a group of armed men surrounded them. Agent Smith started to draw his weapon, but Cynthia stopped him. Mongo had been tracking Cynthia, knowing her next stop would be the cabin.

Anisa came from the side of the cabin and leaned against it. "You know what I like about the mountains? They're free from the chaotic world of people. Why don't we go inside? Someone wants to see you," Anisa suggested as she walked onto the porch. They walked inside. Mona was sitting at the coffee table. While Cynthia was nervous, she knew Mona wouldn't harm her.

"Have a seat," Mona said. "You can leave Agent Smith outside. He's in good hands," Mona assured her. But when Agent Smith refused to move, Mona looked at Anisa who pulled her weapon and shot Smith once in the head; stood over him, shooting three more times.

"Why am I here?" Mona asked her childhood friend.

"I have no idea other than you're looking for your son and Agent Kemp. "I'm on top of it. She'll be in custody soon," Cynthia answered.

Mona began shaking her head. "My people are good at what they do. I found you in the mountains, so we'll eventually find Agent Kemp. I was thinking about a situation that transpired not too long ago. I asked myself, why would Carlos attempt to kill my son? He brought me the head of his only son, guaranteeing a peace treaty. Who would benefit from me being dead? That's the real question." Mona looked at Cynthia and smiled.

"Let me see your hands," Mona said. "Remember the game we used to play when we were kids?"

"Of course!" Cynthia replied as she showed her hands.

"You're shaking. Why would you be so nervous around me? We've known each other our entire lives," Mona reminded her. "Where were you on the day Sky and Kema were attacked?"

"Huh?" Cynthia answered, a bit surprised. "Where are you going with this?"

"Those men who attacked Sky and Kema weren't Cuadras members. Some people went out of their way to make it seem as such. They were private contractors. Here's the thing Cyn," Mona said, referring to her childhood nickname. "I was suppose to be in that car, but there was a change in plans. Sky took my place. Here's the kicker. I had a tracker put on your phone some time ago. And what a coincidence that you were in New York the day the hit went down," Mona explained as the color was sucked out of Cynthia's face.

"Here's the best part of it all. The guys you used were Israelis. You use Israel contractors; the same contractors you used for past missions when the C.I.A. didn't want the other agencies to know about. Don't ask me how I know these things. Just understand that I do."

"It wasn't supposed to happen like that. No one was going to be hurt. I swear it," Cynthia admitted, breaking down in tears.

Anisa swung her gun across Cynthia's head in a violent rage. She was out cold.

Some people have no problem finding what measures create one's demise. So, when you dwell in such territories, make sure that you're willing to go all the way, because some people have all intentions in doing so…

***

Chicago, Illinois
August 4, 2012
9:00 am

Mona granted Yatta access to The Sheridan Corporation, allowing him to transfer funds when instructed. He knew that Mona was wealthy, but to see billions of dollars lying around was baffling. Yatta also handled the laundering of $3.6 billion of company capital.

While Yatta was talking to Capone, Key walked in. "You've been M.I.A. lately. What's up? You hiding something that you don't want me to know about?" Yatta joked.

"I've been spending some time with a good friend. I see Mona got you ripping and running across the country."

"Private jets, five-star hotels, and traveling come with the job. Key, I need you to look into something for me. I got a jump drive out of Peter's safe deposit box, but it's locked. See if your computer guy can unlock it," Yatta said, tossing the jump drive to Key.

"I'll get right on it."

***

Greatfalls, Montana
August 4, 2012
1:19 pm

Cynthia Davis began to regain consciousness as the dizziness wore off. Something was wrong; a sense of danger was in the air. Cynthia became aware of her surroundings, sensing the inevitable. She was on a small commercial airliner heading straight for the mountains. Cynthia panicked as she looked around the plane for anything that would be of use. She ran to the pilots pit and grabbed the controls. They were disabled. The mountains grew closer and closer. Cynthia then looked to the roof of the plane, closed her eyes, and mumbled some prayers. A huge ball of flames and black smoke engulfed the sky as the plane crashed into the mountains. Cynthia died instantaneously.

What you lose in the fire will turn up in the ashes. But in some cases, the fire wins…

Beginning Of The End

Langley, Virginia
August 9, 2012
8:16 am

"Agent Shaw, you have to see this," Agent Bristle said as he dropped an open file on his desk. Both Agents had been assigned to put together a special task force to hunt down Agent Kemp, as well as find holes in Mona's Syndicate. "Cynthia Davis was killed in a plane crash on August 4th one day after Agent Smith was shot dead outside a cabin owned by Cynthia Davis." Agent Shaw listened as things were beginning to take shape.

"Terrence Writter was killed on June 23rd, one day after Cynthia talked with Terrence Writter over the telephone. Then Agent Kemp disappears, taking a target with her. More importantly, why is The Assistant Director of the C.I.A. contacting an F.B.I. case manager?" Agent Bristle added.

"So you think Mona might have Agent Kemp?" Agent Shaw asked.

"I think she's digging in her bag of resources to find Agent Kemp," Agent Bristle replied. "It gets better. There was a shooting in New York on July 17th, leaving one dead and another unknown assailant at large. Our intel says it was Sky, Mona's son. But here's the catch. Cynthia was in the vicinity when the shooting occurred. Liam Shultz of Mona's Syndicate and Israeli Operators were found dead on the scene."

"Hired Contractors?" Skaw asked.

"Yup!" Bristle answers. "Contractors with ties to the C.I.A. And after all this goes down, Cynthia Davis goes on leave and the next thing you know – more bodies. Cynthia and Agent Smith are dead. Oh, did you know that Mona and Cynthia were childhood friends?" Bristle added.

"Whoa! The Assistant Director and Mona Moore had a childhood together and no one cared to share that information?" Agent Shaw was appalled.

"Want to hear my theory?" Agent Bristle asked. "I think Mona had something on Cynthia that allowed her to dictate The Assistant Director's moves, and Cynthia made a play against Mona. But something went wrong. Mona found out and here we are."

"It sounds plausible, but it's all circumstantial. We find Agent Kemp and we got Mona's son," Agent Shaw said.

"What are you suggesting?" Agent Bristle inquired.

"If we hold off on rounding them up, Mona will get careless and make a mistake. Then we make our move," Agent Shaw replied.

"Let's go have a conversation with The Director," Agent Bristle said, as the agents were off to see the man in charge.

***

Chicago, Illinois
August 12, 2012
8:00 pm

Anisa walked into Yatta's home dressed in a sexy, red dress, complimented by her hazel-green eyes. Her hair hung freely pass her shoulders as she walked with an aura of confidence.

"What's the occasion?" Yatta asked as Capone and Deno were into imagining the journey between Anisa's thighs.

"Get dressed in something casual. We're going out. "Would you like to join us," Anisa asked Key. Anisa knew that Key didn't like her, but this wasn't about what she liked. This was business.

Key agreed to go, thinking that she could wear a simple pants suit. No one had seen Key without her hair braided underneath a ball cap. They were impressed, even Anisa, when Key came down the stairs sporting a pants suit tight enough to transform her stud-like persona into that of a seductive vixen. The braids were made into a more sensual look; long, dark hair that brushed pass her shoulders.

"You clean up well," Anisa complimented her.

"Damn! I never thought I would see you in the likes of a feminine woman," Capone said as he approved her transformation.

"Y'all like making me feel really weird. Let's go, so I can change out of these clothes," Key replied.

"Where are we going?" Yatta asked Anisa once they made it down the stairs.

"Club Radius," Anisa answered. "One of their people got killed a while back, so I'm paying his new lieutenant a visit." Capone and Deno never told anyone that they had robbed and killed Q, not even Yatta.

"How do you expect us to get in?" Key asked. "This place is by invitation only!"

"When you're an average person you have those problems. I don't," Anisa said as she got inside the car.

They pulled in front of Club Radius and walked in without any problems. The music was loud; the energy was electric. A-list actors, athletes, rappers, and some important people who played in the underworld were in attendance.

"Key, join me in the ladies room. Yatta, someone is waiting for you in the men's room," Anisa instructed. Once inside, a young woman locked the door and walked towards a stall. Moments later, she emerged with two, forty calibers with attached silencers. They secured their weapons, headed out to meet Yatta. Once the trio regrouped, Anisa explained their next move.

"Key, get us some drinks. We need to blend in. Carlos, leader of The Cuadras Cartel, owns this club. He cleans a lot of money here for his Midwest based operations. There's a count room upstairs with about $20 million of cleaned bills."

"So, we're about to take the money?" Yatta asked.

"No, we're going to destroy it," Anisa replied.

"Twenty-million dollars, we're about to destroy twenty-million dollars?" Yatta asked in disbelief.

"Yes!" Anisa replied. Key arrived with their drinks and took a seat. Anisa went over the plan. There was a ladies room upstairs near the count room by the main office. Anisa and Key headed up the stairs and saw a man standing in front of the count room door. After a few moments in the ladies room, they walked out. The man was gone. The women then walked up another flight of stairs, running into the man they had seen before.

"Can I help you ladies with something? This area is for staff only," the man said, grabbing Anisa by her arm. She turned her charm on, batting her green eyes seductively. Key grabbed Anisa's ass and started to kiss her neck. The man couldn't hide the bulge in his pants that matched his desire to indulge the two beautiful women. Anisa grabbed the man by his tie, pulling him closer.

"Take me somewhere," she said. The man took them to the safe room. Anisa couldn't believe how naïve he was.

"Joey, what the fuck!" One of the men yelled as he opened the heavily bolted door.

"Relax, I brought us two beautiful women," Joey said as Anisa grabbed the man's dick through his pants. One look into her green eyes changed his presence from hesitant to welcoming. Once inside, the door locked behind them. Anisa counted four men, drew her weapon and went to work. Key followed suit, shooting like a seasoned marksman.

"If the two of you want to live, get the fuck on the floor," Anisa yelled. Both men complied.

"You have no idea who you're stealing from," one of the men said.

"Who said anybody was stealing?" Anisa replied, pulling some plastic explosives from her purse. She tossed them on the large table that was filled with stacks of money.

"You guys have a nice day. Key, let's go," Anisa yelled as they left the room. Once outside the door, Anisa shot at the lock, preventing any means of escape for the two men. When Anisa and Key made it downstairs, Yatta joined them.

"Let's go," replied Anisa.

"Why are we leaving?" Yatta pressed for answers. Anisa didn't say a word until they made it back to their car.

"You got the phone?" Anisa asked. When Yatta was told to go to the men's room, he was given a black phone.

"Yeah," Yatta said, removing the phone.

"Dial the numbers eight – two – four," Anisa instructed as they drove away. Once Yatta pressed four, the top level of the club blew up.

"Job done!" Anisa said as she put her shades back on.

Mona came home and found Sky in the living quarters. She had not seen him since the New York tragedy. Although Mona was happy to see that Sky was well and safe, she was unable to openly show her emotions.

"You alright?" Mona asked.

"Yeah, I'm good. Any word on Ty?"

"Nothing yet, but we'll get him back," Mona replied with confidence. "I think you should take some time away from the business," Mona suggested.

"Nawl, I need to work to keep my mind from drifting. Work is good for me right now. Besides, we're short handed as it is," Sky replied. He noticed that Mona had something rolled up in her hand. It was the map she had been working on for a number of years. Sky had no idea what she was up to.

"What's up with you and that map?" Sky asked.

"Asil Anom – you'll understand later," Mona said. Anisa walked in. When Sky saw her, he smiled and thought about Kema. Anisa gave him a hug and looked at Mona.

"It went well," Anisa said as she left to take a shower.

Mourning the death of a loved one can hurt more than the loss. So moving on isn't a bad idea…

***

Chicago, Illinois
August 19, 2012
11:47 pm

Key was sitting on the couch holding the jump drive that Yatta had given her. She knew that any secrets Peter held weren't worth digging up. But Key had killed Peter. Destroying the jump drive would keep her secret buried. Key didn't want her past to tarnish her relationship with Yatta. She had managed to cover her tracks for quite some time. Key got up from the couch and moved into the kitchen. She turned the stove on, sat the jump drive on the burner, and watched it burn without regrets. She then pulled out her phone and called Yatta.

"That jump drive was a dead end. My guy went to decode the encryption, but a virus immediately ate the files. It fried everything," Key explained.

"Fuck! Alright, I'll figure it out," Yatta said, ending the call. Key explored her thoughts while writing on a piece of paper.

Only my Shadow knows the pain,
the struggles in vain
for those who are there.
Besides my Shadow who inhaled
the same recycled air,
who bled as I bled too.
Not ashamed as I cried,
and it cried too.
The Shadow, my voice of reason,
my purpose of being,
the foundation I call home.
My Shadow never left me alone…

Key folded the piece of paper and closed her eyes; believing that she and Keyanna were united into a singular person; loving and protecting her even if it cost Key her life. Keyanna was having problems with a guy named David, an issue Key would deal with at a later time. Key opened her eyes, set fire to the poem and left the kitchen.

***

Miami, Florida
August 23, 2012
2:10 pm

Sky was flying through the streets in his white Bently with Marcella in the passenger seat. Since she had never been to Miami, Sky promised to show her around. They pulled into the parking lot of Ty's boat company.

"This place is huge," Marcella said as she marveled at the yachts and speedboats docked at the pier. The ocean breeze blew her long, sandy-brown hair as she enjoyed the summer sun. "Can we get on a boat?" Marcella asked.

"Pick one," Sky said.

Marcella scanned the room and pointed to a boat near the dock. "That's a nice one, but I prefer yachts," Sky said. "Let's go see my boat." The two of them walked around the back of the boat yard. Marcella's mouth dropped open when Sky pointed to a three-level, mega yacht, complete with a helicopter pad, Jacuzzi, swimming pool and countless amenities.

"It must have cost you a fortune to rent that thing," Marcella said.

"Yeah, good thing I own it," Sky said as he walked onto the deck. Sky enjoyed showing her a good time. After all, she saved his life and preserved his freedom.

The ocean ride was an experience that Marcella would not forget. When they returned to the docks, Sky led Marcella to the parking lot and pointed to a pink and white 911 Porsche Panamera Turbo. "It's yours," Sky said as he tossed a set of keys to her.

Marcella was speechless, overwhelmed with emotion. "Sky, I can't take this from you. I mean, I…"

"It's just a car. Besides, I hate Porsches. It's a girl's car," Sky replied as he cut her off. "Let's go for a drive." Sky slipped into the passenger seat. As Marcella started the car, the evening air was filled with the calming roar of the finely tuned engine, streaking its way up and down the streets of Miami.

Sky noticed a mini-van that seemed to be following them. He studied the car through the rearview mirror. Marcella could see that he was tense. "Sky, what's wrong?"

"Nothing, just drive." Sky replied as he pulled out his gun.

"Sky, you're telling me that nothing is wrong, and now you have a gun in your hand." Marcella was confused by his behavior.

The van moved closer. Sky jumped from the car with gun pointed. About to pull the trigger, he realized it was an elderly woman driving the van. The lady froze, waiting for the impact of gunfire that was about to bring her down. Sky pulled his gun down and jumped back into the Porsche. Marcella didn't say a word as they drove in silence.

"I'm sorry… I thought…I thought…"

"It's okay," Marcella said as she cut him off and grabbed hold of his hand. It was obvious to her that Sky was suffering from the trauma he had experienced while in New York. Sky was losing his battle with paranoia.

If you live in fear for too long, you'll become consumed by the paranoia which bounds you mentally, and that's only the beginning of it. You trap yourself in a world created by your thoughts and killed by the very tools forged in your armory of thoughts. Fear can keep you alive and conscious of your actions, but too much fear devours you in solicitude…

Secrets Revealed

Guadalajara, Mexico
August 29, 2012
1:00 pm

Carlos had a large estate complete with a private airstrip in Guadalarjara, Mexico. He was known as a man who appreciated the finer things in life that only money could provide. It's understandable that he was angry over the $20 million lost in the Club Radius explosion carried out by Anisa and her comrades. Carlos was upset at himself for believing that Mona would honor the peace treaty between the two of them. Mona not only disrespected him, she killed Raul and Paul Mendoza, high officials in the Mendoza Cartel and emissaries of the Cuadras Cartel. Carlos believed their blood was on his hands.

Carlos and his brother, Hector, were talking business. Hector had aspirations of running the family business, wanting to prove himself to Carlos. "The tunnels in El Paso, Texas are nearly complete," Hector said. "We need to pay Ivan a visit about his brothers. Should I go?"

"Not at all," Carlos said. "This is something I have to deal with. You just focus on completing the tunnels. We have a shit load of product, and with the war back on, we need to deal with things accordingly." Carlos released a deep sigh of frustration. "If I had a bomb, I would blow Mona to hell. Then again, she just might be bomb proof."

***

Chicago, Illinois
September 1, 2012
9:45 a.m.

Yatta received a manila envelope from Mona with a letter enclosed. Mona was a mystery, leaving Yatta to still wonder why she trusted him. He unfolded the letter she had written.

> *A lot of items contained in this envelope are things that you'll find heart breaking. You should never have dug up the things in your past. Now you will be left with more unanswered questions. Don't ask me how I know these things that's in the envelope, because it'll only lead to more questions.*
>
> *Mona*

Yatta put the letter down and pulled the contents from the envelope. There were four birth certificates. The first one read – Kenyatta Malik Brown. This revelation alone shocked him, but why would Mona send him a copy of his birth certificate? The next one read – Keyanna Diane Brown. Now Yatta realized that he had a younger sister. Then he read the next one – Nathaniel David Brown. *"What the fuck!"* Yatta thought. *"This can't be right."*

Yatta looked at the attached name change certificates. Malcom Malik Brown was changed to Peter Rosenthal. Yatta was overwhelmed with confusion. According to the documents, Keyanna was his little sister, Nate was his brother that Key killed, and that Peter Rosenthal, killed by an unknown assailant, was his biological father. Yatta put the papers down, punching the table in frustration. He then grabbed a bottle of whiskey from the cabinet.

***

Chicago, Illinois
September 3, 2012
8:16 p.m.

Keyanna made her way through the lobby of the Hilton Hotel, heading towards the elevator. She and Key had made this their spot to hang out. Keyanna sported a pair of tight designer jeans, red bottom heels, and a white blouse that revealed an appropriate amount of her breasts. Her five foot, nine inch well-toned frame was voluptuous; hazel-green eyes complimented her yellow complexion and soft facial features. At 37, her youth remained in full blossom.

When she made it to the hotel room, Keyanna collapsed on the bed. She was having problems with a guy named David, but she lied to Key about her reasons. David was Keyanna's concern and she wanted to keep it that way and wondered how she would deal with him.

***

St. Petersburg, Florida
September 5, 2012
11:19 a.m.

When Yatta arrived at Mona's estate, he found her sitting by the swimming pool. "Let me guess. You have some questions," Mona asked without looking at him or removing her shades. Yatta took a seat next to her and looked at the ground.

"Unfortunately, I do have questions," he admitted. "If Peter was my father, why would he go out of his way to send me to prison?"

"That's a question that only Peter can answer. You chose to open Pandora's box. I warned you. Peter warned you." Mona removed her shades and looked Yatta in the eyes.

"Why do I get the feeling that you knew all of these things prior to bringing me on?" he asked.

"Yatta, I'm no fool. You think I would have brought you on board and not know anything about you? I knew the moment you took Sheridan from Peter. The book you took from Peter containing the names of people he blackmailed, I'm the author of it. I built Sheridan through Peter. He was a politician, the perfect candidate to launch my standings in the realms of corporate America."

Yatta listened in both admiration and disbelief. *This woman is a master of her craft,* he thought.

"Tell me something," Mona asked. "Why do you think I'm so cautious in all endeavors?"

"Trust… Trust is everything," Yatta replied.

"Of course, but not so much that you become vulnerable when you're relaxed and comfortable. Doing so allows your weakness to be exposed. Tell me my weakness?"

Yatta was taken back by her question. He thought of the one thing that his mother would fear – losing her children. "Your sons!" he said.

"Wrong again. Life is there for the taking," Mona paused. "I fear losing power. Power is the most God-like characteristic that man can possess. A balance of paranoia and power creates a level of caution that'll keep you alive. If you fear being shot, then don't make yourself a target."

"So you don't fear losing power, you fear death?" Yatta asked.

"Look into my eyes and ask me, do you see fear?" Mona asked. Yatta was quiet as he sensed a void of emptiness and anger.

"Exactly!" Mona said in response to his silence.

Mona's phone rang. "Hello. I'll be right there." Mona turned her attention back to Yatta. "Let's take a drive."

Yatta found profound meaning in their conversation. "Who is Keyanna?" He asked. "I know she is my sister but where can I find her?"

"This is your puzzle to piece together, not mine. You can drive," Mona said as they headed towards the garage.

Attack At Meddstone

Orlando, Florida
September 9, 2012
12:30 p.m.

Yatta pulled in front of the building and parked as Mona had instructed. Once they made it inside, he was shocked by what he saw. A naked man was hanging from the ceiling by his hands.

"This here is Garcia and he has some things to tell you," Jake said. Jake worked for Mona and distributed drugs to their street networks.

"Why would you bring him to the warehouse?" Mona asked.

"I didn't have any other place to take him," Jake answered.

"Let him down," Mona ordered. Garcia was lowered to the ground. Mona grabbed a chair and sat in front of Garcia.

"What brings you here?" Mona asked the man.

"I'm a tunnel worker for the Mendoza and Cuadras Cartels. They plan on blowing up your oil fields in Texas."

"What tunnels?" Mona asked.

"We're building a tunnel network to traffic drugs underneath the border and up to El Paso," Garcia answered.

"When is the attack going to happen?" Mona asked

"I don't know when, but it's soon," he answered.

"Why are you coming to us with this information?" Mona inquired.

"The Mendoza Cartel killed my entire family and I want revenge." After studying Garcia's facial expressions, Mona believed him to be the man he was posing to be. But then, Mona grabbed his hands. "You have very nice hands." She complimented. He didn't reply. Yatta noticed the look in Mona's eyes.

Yatta picked up a large pipe and swung it across Garcia's head. The second blow put him down, permanently.

"Get him out of here," Mona told Jake. When Jake bent over to drag Garcia out of the room, Mona pulled her gun and shot him in the head. Garcia's hands were too soft to be a tunnel worker; his skin was too oiled to be a drug mule; and his name wasn't Garcia. Mona read the trap easily and understood the logic as to why he went through hell to gain her loyalty.

Carlos was clever, but not enough. You can persuade someone with the truth to gain their trust, but when you tangle lies with honesty, the objective falls short. Mona made a few calls to dispose of the bodies and left the building.

"How did you know that I wanted you to kill him?" Mona asked.

"I didn't!" Yatta replied and got inside the car. Mona smiled in approval.

***

Chicago, Illinois
September 11, 2012
11:19 p.m.

Key and Keyanna entered the Hilton Hotel and slipped into David's room, a room two doors from theirs. Although Key was leading the way, Keyanna dictated their movements. It was obvious that Keyanna had a strong influence on Key's behavior. Being a light sleeper, David woke when the door opened.

"What are you doing in my room?" David said as he looked for his glasses. After putting on the glasses, the image became clear – it was Keyanna.

"Shoot him… Shoot him…" Keyanna said. Her words danced in Key's head, trying to process why Keyanna wanted David killed. Earlier, Keyanna told her that there was a problem with David, but that was all she said. Following her instructions, Key pointed the gun at David's head; his hands reached high.

"Keyanna, you're sick. Let me help you. Please, you don't want to do this," David said. His pleading was in vain. Key pulled the trigger and shot him dead.

***

Dallas, Texas
September 15, 2012
8:39 a.m.

Anisa's jet landed on a private airstrip near the Meddstone Headquarters. Her men were on location prior to her arrival; given instructions that Anisa and Mona would take care of things.

Anisa's phone rang. "The last I saw you, you had no use for me. Now I'm on a jet heading your way – this time to Dallas," Yatta replied with a touch of humor. "I have to make sure that everything is good."

"Do you mean I should be prepared for the worst?" Anisa laughed. She had taken a liking to Yatta, which was rare. "You should always be prepared with me. My job requires me to handle bad things. I'll see you when you get here," Anisa said as she hung up.

Anisa entered a large two-story house located on the edge of the airstrip. It had been a long day and the thought of a shower felt right. Anisa walked to the second floor, pulled the shirt over her head, stripped down to nothing, and stepped into the shower. The hot water caused her muscles to relax as she enjoyed the moment. While Anisa lathered her head with a sweet smelling shampoo, she heard the wooden stairs on the first floor make a creating sound, as if someone was walking across the floor. She turned the water off, pulled the shower curtain back, and stepped from the shower stall. Anisa knew to assume an assailant might be downstairs. With haste, she put on her bra and panties. She had told her men to stand guard on the Meddstone properties, wondering who could possibly be on the lower level. Anisa made it to the other room and put the Kevlar over her torso, and grabbed her weapons. There was no time to add more clothing -- a bra, panties, and her bulletproof vest.

As soon as she made it to the hallway, a shot rang out. Anisa ducked and returned fire. She then slid on the other side of the wooden post and fired two more rounds. A body could be heard rolling down the stairs. Anisa walked to the stairway and looked down. She had to make it downstairs. The uncertainty made her heart pound hard and fast.

Anisa stepped onto the main floor. The front door flew open followed by rapid gunfire. She ducked behind a wooden bookcase and saw two men enter the house carrying assault rifles. The men took different paths. Anisa then crawled around the couch and rolled under the coffee table. One man crept around the couch, thinking that he had the drop on her. But Anisa wasn't there. The man back peddled and felt a metal object being shoved into his crotch. **Psst! Psst!** A bullet followed the two shots to his head.

Anisa rolled from under the table, and fired two shots at the other man.

Psst!

Psst!

He fell to his knees; Anisa put him down. When she stood, there was a third man totting a shotgun.

Boom!

The impact of the 12-guage blew her across the room and against the wall. The air was sucked from her body, causing her to pull the Kevlar apart, allowing her to breathe. Several men entered the room and surrounded her.

***

Dallas, Texas
September 15, 2012
9:00 a.m.

Yatta had just landed in Dallas, only a short distance from Anisa's location. There was so much chaos in his personal life that he welcomed a temporary distraction. How could he find Keyanna; how could he tell her that she was his sister? Perhaps a private investigator would be a realistic option. In a weird way, prison was more manageable than his life as a free man.

***

Dallas, Texas
September 15, 2012
9:00 a.m.

The bulletproof vest saved her life, but the pain was ongoing. Hector, high official in the Cuadras Cartel, took a seat on the couch, giving Anisa time to gather herself. One of Hector's men kicked Anisa in the ribs, causing her to cough up blood and gasp for air.

"You killed a lot of my men," Hector said. "For a beautiful woman, you have a violent reputation. But I do applaud your commitment to Mona." He walked up to Anisa and squatted near her, brushing a strand of hair from her face.

Anisa spit a glob of blood in his face. "Fuck you!" she said with a sinister smile.

Hector laughed. "I can't kill you. The boss has something in store for you," Hector said as he knocked her out. Anisa was then loaded into a white van.

***

Dallas, Texas
September 15, 2012
9:30 a.m.

Yatta was around the corner from Anisa's location. As the driver made a turn, they nearly collided with the speeding white van. The driver waved his hand as if to say he was sorry, and continued to speed. When Yatta made it to his destination, the driver popped the trunk and handed Yatta an assault rifle. They stepped over the bodies in the house as they searched for Anisa. She was nowhere to be found. Yatta pulled out his cell phone and called Mona. "We got a problem. Anisa's gone and we got a house full of dead people."

Peace Treaty Gone Bad

St. Petersburg, Florida
September 16, 2012
9:00 a.m.

Mona was certain that Carlos had Anisa and she wasn't dead. Mona contacted Sky and broke the news of Anisa's disappearance. Mona loved her like a daughter and would do anything to bring her home. Although she suffered internally, she held it together for the sake of the Syndicate. It's expected when you're the CEO of a multi-billion dollar organization.

Mona made the call to Carlos. "Where is she?" Mona asked with a stern voice.

"Well, hello to you," Carlos answered. "I'll say this, the girl killed a lot of men on her way down." Carlos knew Anisa was Mona's tactician and trusted enforcer.

"You broke our arrangement and killed two important men that weren't suppose to die," Carlos said. "That's all your doing, not mine.

"That was a misunderstanding," Mona said. "My son and an associate were attacked in New York. Someone made it seem as if they were your people." As Mona explained things to Carlos, he was shocked that Cynthia Davis would go that far to create a feud.

"That doesn't change the fact that blood has been spilled. What should we do to call it even?" Carlos asked.

"Let's talk face to face," Mona suggested.

"You're a passionate woman, that I admit. But I can't let this go unresolved. So, I have an idea. Once I kill Anisa, I'll give her a proper burial. That's the least I could do."

"If you touch one strand on her head, I'll erase every drop of your bloodline breathing and leave you alive long enough to mourn their death," Mona threatened.

"The people I loved died in relations to the game we both play. I lost my wife and I killed my son to advance in this game. If my house burns down, then so does yours."

"I'll see you soon!" Mona said, slamming the phone against the wall. She had Mango tracking Agent Kemp, so this was a job for someone else. Carlos would feel her wrath.

***

Juarez, Mexico
September 19, 2012
Time – Unknown

Anisa was nodding in a state of euphoric bliss. Hector had been shooting her up with pure heroin for the past two days. The drugs removed all feelings, allowing her to survive the sexual abuse and beatings.

Anisa was being held in a barn-like structure. The man guarding Anisa gave her and himself an injection of heroin. He then lit a cigarette and enjoyed the peace that drugs offer. The guard passed out, allowing the cigarette to ignite the bails of hay. Anisa smelled smoke as the fire spread across the floor and into the walls. The heat encased the barn.

"Anisa... Anisa ... Look at me," Kema seemed to call out.

Anisa recognized Kema's voice. "You're dead," Anisa replied.

"You have to get up, you can't stay here," the imaginary voice continued.

"I'm tired. Just want to sleep," Anisa said as she closed her eyes.

"Anisa, we're running out of time," Kema said.

Kema screamed, "Anisa!"

She then snapped out of her unconsciousness and looked for Kema. She wasn't there. Anisa felt her skin begin to boil. The roof collapsed.

***

Orlando, Florida
September 20, 2012
9:15 p.m.

Carlos decided to attend a masquerade party thrown by Fernando Mendoza. Fernando was the brother of Ivan Mendoza and the second in command of the Mendoza Cartel. While Ivan was in Federal custody, Fernanda ran the Cartel. The death of his younger brothers hit him hard, but it was the nature of the business. The guests were dressed for the occasion and the music shook the building.

Several men walked through the entrance dressed in black suits, wearing white masks. They walked in military formation guarding a woman dressed in a white cat suit with a black mask. As they walked pass Fernando and Carlos, Carlos grabbed her hand.

"You've got to be someone important with such a grand entrance," Carlos said. The woman didn't speak.

"Would you like to join me and my friend for a drink? Your body guards can stand watch over you if you like," Fernando said. While she didn't speak, she accepted his offer of a few drinks. Carlos grabbed a few women to entertain him, leaving the quiet lady to Fernando. Fernando's men stood outside of his private cubical and didn't allow anyone pass the red ropes. The silent woman took a drink from Fernando and sat across from Carlos who paid her no attention. Fernando fondled the woman's breast as he invited her into the cubicle.

"Can I get your name?" Fernando asked.

"It depends," the woman said as she continued to watch Carlos.

"Depends on what," Fernando asked.

"How much you're willing to do for a name!" the woman replied. "I don't like to get that personal," the quiet woman's voice had a sensuous tone.

"Well, maybe we should get out of here and go somewhere more comfortable," Fernando suggested.

"Maybe," she continued to tease.

"How about this, you give me your name and I'll make it worth your time," Fernando said.

"Mona!" she replied, taking her mask off. Fernando had the look of horror on his face. Carlos' eyes grew as he struggled to find his breath as if God himself had snatched it from his lungs. While Mona's men drew their weapons, Fernando's men had no idea what was taking place.

"Carlos, you know why I'm here. Where is she?" Mona demanded.

"How do you expect to make it out of here alive?" Carlos replied.

"We'll cross that bridge once we get there. Now where is she? I'm not going to ask again," Mona said.

"She's in an old dairy farm in Juarez. You probably don't want to see her right now. She's, let's say, not herself," Carlos said in a humorous tone that Mona did not find funny. She pulled two grenades from her purse and pulled the pins.

"What the fuck is wrong with you?" Fernando yelled. Mona put one live grenade under each of their thighs.

"I wouldn't move if I was you," Mona said as she put her mask back on and walked out of the cubicle.

***

Colima, Mexico
September 21, 2012
2:06 a.m.

Anisa was found nearly a week ago on the streets of Juarez, Mexico; the most dangerous place in the world. Just this year alone, the Cartels and local gangs were accountable for some thousand homicides. Anisa's left side from head to toe was damaged from the fire. The entire right side of her body was untouched, even her long, dark hair still hung freely.

An elderly woman who transported cattle from Nogales and Hermosillo through Juarez found Anisa on the streets. Since Anisa's condition had the Cartel written all over her, nobody wanted to be seen helping her. The elderly woman put Anisa in her truck and took her to Colima, Mexico. Anisa was holding on to the small bit of life she had left. Time was running out.

***

Juarez, Mexico
September 21, 2012
2:30 a.m.

When they arrived at the old dairy farm, it was nothing but ashes. Finding it was not the problem. Juarez wasn't a place where you could roam around easily. Even Mona, a woman of stature had to know someone familiar with the streets of Juarez. Mona had her men go through every board and piece of rubble, looking for Anisa's body. While they did find a charred body, it wasn't her. Anisa was a fighter, and as long as she was still alive, there was hope. Maybe she could figure something out and return to her home. Mona didn't have the answers, but she knew the strength and determination of Anisa.

If you fear being shot, then don't make yourself a target. Adversity can bring a set of problems that'll demand the best from you. It's either that or you can just roll over and die…

***

Chicago, Illinois
September 29, 2012
3:45 p.m.

Yatta put Key and Deno in one of Mona's safe houses used to ship dirty bills for laundering. Somehow, the house had been made and robbed. Although the majority of the money had been transferred to the Sheridan Corporation, this was about the principle.

Six men sat on the corner of 89th and State Street. Although this was quite a distance from the stash house, the streets told a tale that brought Key and the entourage here. The men watched as a black Benz and white Audi pulled up to the corner. Deno and Capone emerged from the vehicles and approached the men.

"My Nigga – Y'all lost or something?" One of the men barked. Once Capone got close, he hit the man in the jaw and pulled out his gun. Deno followed suit. The man Capone hit took off. Once he put some distance between himself and Capone he turned and yelled, "I'll see you bitch ass nigga --- word. I'm big black dawg, and I run these fucking streets." As he turned around, Key appeared and swung her gun across his face and he fell to the ground.

Boom!

Boom!

His brains leaked out of his head, painting the pavement red. Capone turned to the other men that they held up. He had their attention. "That house you all robbed, don't let that happen again. Next time y'all house might come up missing with everybody in it," Capone said.

Anisa On The Mend

New York, New York
October 1, 2012
9:00 am

Sky and Marcella had grown close and were spending a lot of time together. Sky was skeptical about coming back to New York because of the shoot out that had transpired. Mona's contacts advised her that there was nothing that indicated or tied him to the shootings. But Sky couldn't help but be concerned. While the thought of Kema's death was crushing, he had to move on.

Marcella had moved into a larger apartment. As Sky helped her pack, he found an old sweater that made him laugh. "You actually wear this shit?" Sky laughed while holding up a Leapord sweater.

"Of course, my nana made it for me," Marcella replied as she snatched the sweater from Sky. He picked up a photo album and opened it. The first person he saw was Soria. Marcella offered to explain who he was looking at.

"That's my mother, Soria," she said.

"You two really favor each other," Sky complimented. He had never told her that he knew her mother, and had conducted business with her on numerous occasions.

What a small word," Sky thought. "We're polar opposites. She lives in a world that'll eat me alive on my best day. She's more free hearted that I am."

Marcella loved her mother, but was not fond of the underground world and the ugly things that came with it. He admired Marcella and her drive to want something better out of life rather than living in her mother's shadow. "Grab the stuff you can't live without and let's just go on a shopping spree. Just one condition," Sky said

"And what might that be?" Marcella asked.

"You have to let me burn this sweater," Sky said while snatching the Leapord sweater from her and ran to the stove. Marcella gave chase in protest and playfully tackled him to the floor. The two of them finished packing. Sky had to make a run.

"I'll meet up with you later," Sky said. "If you need anything, give me a call."

"Be careful out there," Marcella replied with a bit of concern in her voice.

"I'll do my best," Sky replied.

***

Minneapolis, Minnesota
October 4, 2012
10:37 a.m.

Yatta and his son, Lil J, were breaking sweat while playing a game of one-on-one basketball. As the game came to an end, Brittany stood in her door way and watched their bonding moment. She and Yatta were becoming friends.

"You're pretty good with your son," Brittany said as Lil J ran to his house to take a shower.

"Yeah, he's just growing up so fast," Yatta replied, leaning against the fence.

"Wish I could spend more time with my daughter, but my job keeps me on the road." I'm a travel agent Brittany said.

"That must be nice, being able to travel around the country," Yatta commented.

"Yeah, that's a plus that comes with the job," Brittany said.

Yatta's phone rang. "Mona, what's up?" Yatta answered as Agent Kemp (Brittany) turned and walked into the house. Agent Kemp, also known as Olivia – Ty's personal assistant, heard Mona's name and began to panic. She ran into the room and strapped on her vest and grabbed her weapons. She then ran to check on Ty who remained stable. Kemp looked out the window and saw Yatta get in his car and drive away.

Perhaps Agent Kemp was too paranoid and Yatta was on the phone with a different Mona. A thousand thoughts raced through Kemp's mind, making it difficult to weigh her options. She pulled the van around back near the ramp. She had an evacuation plan in case of a situation like this. She had never seen Yatta prior to her cover being blown or heard from any of the brothers speak of him. It took her fifteen minutes and she was ready to go.

"I got you," Agent Kemp said to Ty as she pulled out of the driveway.

You can only run for so long. Eventually, you'll run out of real estate.

***

Colima, Mexico
October 6, 2012
9:00 a.m.

Anisa was twisted into a fetal position, sweating and shaking, as her bed-ridden body fought for normalcy in a drug-addicted world.

"Anisa, don't follow the light. Stay away from it," Kema appeared to have said.

Anisa saw an ambience of light surrounding Kema, and smiled. "Where else am I to go?" Anisa imagined, moving toward Kema. The monitor that recorded the heart rate and pulse began to beep at a rapid pace. The elderly woman and her two daughters ran into the room and went to work.

"Anisa, go back," Kema seemed to say. Anisa reached for Kema's hand as the light grew more intense.

The elderly woman knew what Anisa's body needed, but was reluctant to give into it. Anisa was about to go into shock as the withdrawals were causing her body to shut down. The woman knew it might come to this and was prepared. "Get me the black purse from my bedroom table," she told her daughter. As the daughter returned with the purse, the woman removed a syringe and administered an injection of heroin into Anisa's drug-starved body.

***

Miami, Florida
October 8, 2012
9:36 p.m.

Mona invited Yatta to lunch, wanting to show her appreciation. Most people would have kept their distance had they known the Federal government was targeting their employer. "You can go a long way with me and become a wealthy man. You have a strong will," Mona complimented him.

"The money is part of the cycle," Yatta said. "I like being in a position to take care of my family." While Mona's world was crumbling around her and the problems were increasing, her aura was humble and poised.

"Do you have any kids?" Mona asked.

"Yeah, I have a son. He's nearly grown," Yatta said as he pulled out his phone. While sliding through the photos, one caught Mona's eye, causing her to grab Yatta's arm.

"Go back. Who is that woman?" Mona asked. Yatta had a picture from three weeks ago. Lil J had taken a picture of himself while playing around in the yard. Brittany was in the background.

"Oh, that's just my neighbor, Brittany," Yatta said as he passed the phone to Mona.

She blew the photo up and turned to Yatta. "That's Agent Kemp," Mona said while pulling out her cell phone. "Mongo – she's in Minnesota!"

***

Colima, Mexico
October 8, 2012
9:40 p.m.

While Anisa's health was improving, she continued to fight through her addition to heroin. The elderly woman's name was Rosita. Her daughters were Anna and Rosie. Her youngest daughter Rosie, had learned how to care for people from her mother who was a nurse. Rosita had the compassion to help people. She knew that Mexico was home to some of the most dangerous criminals in the world, but there were a lot of good people too.

The Cartels had a stranglehold on Mexico, turning it into a war zone. While Rosita was clueless to what Anisa had done, it didn't warrant the level of torture she had endured. Rosita was amazed at how one side of Anisa's body was untouched by the fire. Rosita continued to inject small amounts of heroin into Anisa's I.V. It's what kept Anisa alive. Anisa was unresponsive, but her heart was pumping in overtime to strengthen her battle against the drugs. Anisa had turned the corner. She wanted to live.

Hatred could be more than motivating. It could will you further than anything in this world…

Safe House

Neuquen, Argentian
October 8, 2012
9:55 p.m.

Fernando had a contact in Neuquen, Argentina who cooked the highest quality of meth known to the underworld. Fernando convinced Carlos to go to Neuquen, Argentian and check out a man known as "the meth cooker."

"They call me 'the cook,' not because of my method, but by my process and the compromise I take with my cooking. What do you know about meth?" he asked.

"It sells better than sex," Carlos joked.

"Of course it does," the man said. "Methamphetamine is a central nervous system stimulant drug; the same as amphetamine. The drug is a white, odorless, bitter-tasting crystalline powder that dissolves in water or alcohol, and is taken orally, snorting the powder through the nasal passage, injection or smoking."

"What's your point?" Carlos inquired.

"I know everything there is to know about meth. It increases the release and blocks the reuptake of the brain chemical or neurotransmitter –

dopamine – leading to high levels of the chemical in the brain. I found a way to balance the process it takes to cook the drug at levels that bypasses the standards we know as pure."

Now Carlos was intrigued. "Keep talking," Carlos urged.

"Most crystal meth cooks have labs based in Mexico. Mexican super meth is dominating the markets and you rarely find other countries that can compete with them -- until now. That was because the United States has restrictions on the main ingredients used to make crystal meth. One in particular would be the drug called pseudoephedrine."

"Let's talk in layman terms," Carlos said.

"I have black ice. The crystal comes out black and is ten times greater than the standard purity levels known any where in the world."

"Production – How much of this can you produce," Carlos asked as the cook responded with a belly laugh.

"Four hundred pounds a week, maybe more," the cook answered.

"I'll see you in Juarez," Carlos said. Just like that, black crystal would soon be on the streets of foreign soil.

***

Minneapolis, Minnesota
October 8, 2012
11:40 p.m.

Agents Bristle and Shaw walked into the house that Agent Kemp had fled, and saw that the front and back doors had been breached. "This was the work of a professional. The doors had been breached at an angle to minimize the noise and create a clean break," Agent Shaw explained. They had the crime scene technicians dusting the place and so far, there wasn't much of a story to be told.

"Somebody went out of their way to wipe this place clean. Why go through such a task?" Agent Bristle questioned.

"Because it leaves no trace of a trail to follow," Agent Shaw replied as he walked outside to look around. He saw old tire tracks in the grass and a second set of fresher tracks. "She's running. Who ever came for her was too late, leaving no sign of a struggle, blood, or any sign of a disturbance," Agent Shaw said while walking away.

"How do you know that Agent Kemp isn't dead?" Agent Bristle asked.

"Because she would never have switched her locator on here. She's leaving us a trail to follow," Agent Shaw replied as they left the scene.

***

Mexico
Location Unknown
Federal Holding Compound
October 11, 2012
9:16 a.m.

Ivan Rubio Mendoza was being held in one of Mexico's most secured facilities in the country. There was no official address. Visitors were put on a bus with no visibility or sense of direction that led to the facility. Carlos hated visiting prisons. But this was necessary, and more so out of respect. When Carlos made it to the visiting room, his old friend greeted him. "Longtime my brother," Ivan said as they embraced.

"I can never get used to seeing you bound in chains, even after fifteen years. How are you?" Carlos asked.

"Besides the obvious circumstances, I'm living. So, ain't much to complain about. A man bound in chains is only as free as a man locked inside his head. You learn to live outside your circumstances, that's when you're truly free," Ivan replied.

"You're a gentle man and I value our friendship. You know if I'm here it's for a reason," Carlos said.

"I know already and it didn't come from Fernando. Word travels fast and the deaths of my brothers were no secret. The nature of the business is hunt or be hunted. We both have taken similar loses," Ivan said.

"Sadly we have," Carlos replied. "My business with Mona will continue until one of us is dead," Carlos spoke with conviction.

"Don't allow your desire to over shadow your ambition. Irrational thoughts only lead to bad decisions. Think! Wits win battles and conquer wars. My time is up. You take care of yourself," Ivan said, standing ready to return to his cell.

When you feel pain it means that you're capable of feeling discomfort. But the moment the pain stops, is the moment you find nothing…

***

Fort Smith, Canada
October 17, 2012
9:00 a.m.

Agent Kemp called some people outside the agency whom she trusted. They put her up in Fort Smith, Canada. For now, the running was over. Still, she knew that Mona would never stop coming for Ty and putting her in a grave. Agent Kemp was going through a lot of mental stress added to the fact that she missed her daughter. But Kemp wouldn't stop running until she was ready to come in.

The house Agent Kemp used was away from the main roads and civilization. The population was about two thousand closely-knit people who could be described as good, ordinary folks. Out of caution, Kemp created an evacuation plan, making sure she was prepared in case trouble came knocking.

Ty's condition had not made any significant progress. She made arrangements for a doctor to see him. The doctor said Ty's brain activity was good, and that time would improve his responsiveness.

There are two wolves that live within us. The one you feed the most is the wolf that'll survive…

Business As Usual

Reno, Nevada
October 26, 2012
12:19 a.m.

Sky was sitting at his desk going over the books and Vino's audit. The Royal Diamond Casino and Resort was doing well. The business side of the world didn't mourn the deaths of loved ones. The Royal Diamond Casino and Resort, and Meddstone Drilling were their safeguards and the most lucrative assets. All of the street capital was laundered and cleaned for other ventures that kept them legit.

While Sky was on the phone a woman walked into his office. "You're a long way from home aren't you?" Sky asked Soria. Like Marcella, her mother, Soria, was a beautiful woman. Her long, jet-black hair was holstered in a ponytail, and her light brown eyes welcomed the ogling gazes of men who pursued her attention.

"When duty calls I answer. I had business in Vegas, so I decided to pay you a visit," Soria said as she took a seat.

"I'm flattered for the visit but I know it's not the reason you are in town. So, what brings you here?" Sky preferred straight talk.

"Vino and I had an arrangement that I wish to keep in place. I own a club in Vegas and use both companies to launder our capital in large sums, much faster. Working together would prove lucrative for both sides," Soria said.

"I would honor whatever arrangements you had with Vino," Sky assured her. Soria smiled.

"How is Mona?" she asked.

"She's well"

"Whenever you find yourself in Colombia, give me a call," Soria said.

"Why would I be in Columbia?" Sky asked.

"Because my daughter always visits her Grandmother for her birthday," Soria replied, leaving Sky looking dumb founded.

***

Dallas, Texas
October 30, 2012
8:08 a.m.

"Our last meeting we had a discussion about buying into the oil rigs in the Pacific Ocean. Well, Exxon-Mobile agreed to sell at $110 Billion. That includes the other two rigs located in the Atlantic Ocean as well. All three rigs have a projected growth of $300 Billion in Capital," Jasmine Lockhart explained.

"In what time span would we expect a return of our investment?" Mona inquired.

"In three to five years – six tops," Janice Lockhart interjected.

"How many investors do we have on board?" Sky inquired.

"Our proposal hasn't been presented to any of the prospected investors." Jasmine replied.

"What about the solar panel projects?" Sky wanted to know.

"The company who was producing the solar panels, they pulled out. They said the overhead cost and shipping wasn't part of the contract," explained Janice.

"Whose responsible for the panels being produced?" Mona asked.

"Our Ireland investors," Sky answered.

"Did he pull out or decided to discontinue the funding," Mona asked as she was beginning to feel anger.

"His name is John Walsh. He said to finance someone else's company with no real body of work outside of oil investments would be economical suicide," Janice added.

"Can we find another company to use until our lawyers redo the contracts?" Asked Mona.

"We will look around," Jasmine assured her.

"Whatever the cost for the overhead and shipping may amount to, I'll fund it until we deal with the contracts." Mona left the room.

She took her phone out and called Yatta. "I may need a hand with something."

***

New York, New York
November 1, 2012
1:00 a.m.

Sky took Marcella out for dinner. He felt it best not to tell Marcella that he saw her mother, let alone that Soria knew they were friends. Sky was still a bit upset over the fact that Marcella had a black eye and wouldn't tell him who did it; he had no use for a man who hits a woman. Marcella was protecting Sky from doing something stupid that he would later regret. She had broken off a relationship with a man named Jason.

When they returned to Marcella's place, Sky fell asleep on the leather recliner. Sky opened his eyes as he felt the presence of someone standing over him. It was Marcella wrapped in a bath towel. Sky was reluctant to cross any lines that would spoil their friendship. She was like the little sister he never had. He couldn't deny the fact that he was attracted to her, but that was beside the point. Sky sat up, intending to protest her intentions.

"Let's not cro…" She hushed him by putting her finger over his lips.

"Let me have this moment," she whispered. When Marcella dropped her towel, Sky closed his eyes. Marcella grabbed his face. "Look at me – please." Sky gave in to his desires. Marcella moved onto his lap and began kissing his lips. From there, all lines were crossed.

***

Waterford, Ireland
November 3, 2012
6:00 p.m.

John Walsh was an executive for a clean energy company called APT Corporation. He had pledged a substantial amount of capital towards the funding of Meddstone's energy project. But then he pulled out of the deal. Mona was not happy about John's withdrawal, and he was about to find out.

Mona and Key were escorted to John's office and were greeted by a pleasant smile on John's face. "I'm sorry you had to fly this far, but unfortunately my position hasn't changed. My decision is final."

"I have more than $500 Million invested in this projected, a decision that was based on your commitment," Mona explained.

"That kind of money is nothing to sneeze at, but unfortunately people on my end aren't willing to invest. When I originally agreed to the terms, I was wrong for doing so. At the time, I spoke for all of the players and they didn't agree with my decision. I'm sorry Ms. Moore."

"Mr. Walsh, in the business world, your word is supposed to be your bond."

"Ms. Moore, maybe I'm not making myself clear. There is nothing to discuss, so you're now wasting my time," He said, cutting her off.

"I see. Key, let's go," Mona replied, shaking John's hand on her way out.

***

Minneapolis, Minnesota
November 3, 2012
7:45 p.m.

Yatta had sent Key to accompany Mona on a trip to Ireland. He believed that Key needed a vacation away from everything going on here. She hadn't been herself lately, causing Yatta to wonder what was going on. Yatta wanted to see Tasha who was dealing with some personal problems. After the ordeal with Agent Kemp being their neighbor and Mongo nearly turning their home into a crime scene, it reminded Yatta that bad things could find its way to their home.

"You're back in town early?" Tasha asked while Yatta entered their home.

"I thought since I had some free time, why not spend it at home," he replied, taking his jacket off.

"You're up to something," Tasha spoke with a suspicious tone.

"What – you want me to leave?" Yatta asked as he approached her, sliding his hands under her shirt. She didn't have a bra on. The touch of his hands made her nipples turn hard.

"Noooo!" She said with little resistance. He pulled the shirt over her head, slid her panties down, and stuck his fingers into the folds of her womb. Tasha sighed in pleasure, pulled at his jeans, helping him undress. His penis gained an erection, followed by Tasha lubricating his shaft with the semen seeping from his head. Yatta pushed her onto the couch as she held her legs up, inviting him to enter her fold. He slowly penetrated her as she dug her nails into his back. She began to sing in sensuous sounds of pleasure, driving him to pound harder. She arched her back as she matched his strides, feeling a rush between her legs, an exploding sensation.

Yatta told her to turn around. She complied with eagerness as the cum ran down her legs. As he stroked her, she felt his erection deep into her mid section. She moved her hand behind, trying to slow him down. But Yatta smacked her hand and continued with a mixture of short and long strokes. Tasha began throwing herself at him, taking his strides with ease. Yatta exploded inside her and collapsed. Tasha then pushed him off and walked to the shower.

***

Waterford, Ireland
November 3, 2012
9:16 p.m.

John Walsh had picked his wife and daughter up from their house, heading for a night out. John took pride in being the breadwinner in the family and taking care of his girls. His daughter, Amber, was 15 and a typical teenager. John's wife, Carol, was his childhood crush and their happiness had continued throughout their marriage.

"So, what movie should we see tonight?" John asked.

"I want to see *Fifty Shades Darker*," Carol said

"Don't you think that might be a bit too much for Amber?" John asked.

"Dad, I'm not a kid," she spoke in protest.

"How about we go see *Ghost in a Shell*, you know, the movie with Scarlett Johansson," John suggested. Then, out of nowhere, they crashed into the back of a white truck. John's car spun out of control and crashed into a ditch. He was momentarily dazed, then turned to check on his family.

"Is everybody alright?" he asked.

"Yeah, I'm fine," Carol replied, seeing that Amber was fine as well.

The driver of the white truck jumped the guardrail and ran to their car. "Are you guys okay?" Key inquired.

"Yeah, you should be more careful. You could have seriously hurt one of us," John said as he looked up. "I know you. You're one of Ms. Moore associates," John said

"Yeah, I am," Key said, pulling her gun. John eyes grew as panic set in. His protest had no chance. Key shot him dead and sent his family with him.

When death comes knocking, make sure the door is locked, even the windows…

Breach!

St. Petersburg, Florida
November 5, 2012
4:00 p.m.

"Team one in position!"
"Team two in position!"
"Team three in position!"

The agents watched from their mobile command center as the breach teams prepared to enter Mona's estate. The C.I.A. and F.B.I. decided to bring Mona in for questioning. While most of the evidence they had against her was circumstantial, they believed it was worth taking a shot, hoping she might make a mistake during intake and talk. No matter the cost, they had to take Mona off the streets.

"Breach!" The order was given and explosives went off as the teams stormed the estate in tactical fashion. To their surprise, Mona was waiting for them. She was drinking red wine by the pool with her lawyers in attendance.

"What took you so long?" Mona mocked them and smiled.

The teams surrounded her. "Suspect in Custody," they called in as they cuffed her. Mona's lawyers followed her all the way to lock up and advised her not to say a word. The agents started tearing through her house and wasted no time in doing so. They confiscated all her computers and laptops. Mona had wiped them clean, and the agents knew it. They found nothing.

"She's smart, if I must say so," Agent Shaw admitted.

"What do you think of this? She attempted to burn this, but wasn't successful," Agent Bristle said as he pulled a piece of a map from the fireplace.

"She didn't destroy it completely, she wanted us to find it. She's toying with us," replied Agent Shaw, who left the house and drove away.

***

Sky was watching the news as it covered what had transpired at Mona Moore's estate. Things were turning to shit. There weren't any formal charges filed yet, but when the Feds have their hands in the mix, no telling what could happen.

Anisa was missing and Kema was dead. Ty was in a coma and absent as well. Now Sky would have to keep the organization afloat by himself. Sky knew Mona wouldn't get a bond due to her abundance of resources and financial stability. He had to meet with Yatta and begin putting things into perspective. The worse was yet to come. They still had to deal with the Cuadras Cartel and this time, something had to give.

When the rain comes down, some things just can't avoid getting wet…

***

Williston, North Dakota
Women's Federal Holding Facility
November 6, 2012
12:04 a.m.

"You're a very slippery woman Ms. Moore," Agent Shaw said, tapping his pen on the table. "Where is Agent Kemp?" he asked.

"You mean to tell me that the man on the other side of that glass can't find his own Agent? Wow," she said and smiled.

"You don't think that we know you had Cynthia and Agent Smith killed?" Mona's lawyer, Erin Crossfalls, interrupted Agent Shaw.

"This meeting is over," Attorney Crossfalls said as the door opened and he stormed in. "We have invoked our client's right to remain silent during her booking, and this badgering is a clear deprivation of my client's constitutional rights. I will be sure to file a formal complaint and speak with your superiors," Erin Crossfalls spoke with authority.

"You know you're not getting out of this," Agent Shaw said as he looked at Mona.

"I never shy away from threats. You're a smart man, and should know that," replied Mona.

"Keep that demeanor," Agent Shaw said.

"Tell Amy I said hello and don't be late picking Gwendolyn up from piano practice," Mona advised.

"You go anywhere near my family and I will fucking destroy you," Agent Shaw snapped and walked out of the room. Mona smiled, staring at the double-sided mirror.

"They don't build prisons that can hold women like me, Mr. Director."

***

Miami, Florida
November 9, 2012
8:27 p.m.

Sky pulled into the shipping yard, proceeding towards the docks. Since Mona's arrest, Sky started prepping himself to deal with things his way. He not only had to run the family affairs, he needed to tie up the loose ends, keeping Mona safe from prosecution by the federal government. Erin

Crossfalls told Sky that that there was another confidential informant providing information to Agent Shaw.

Sky walked down to the docks and found Benny tied to a chair. Benny was the bookkeeper for the boat company and was familiar with the money laundering activities within the company. Sky knew that Benny met with the Feds and wanted to know why.

"Who did you meet with two weeks ago Benny?" Sky asked.

"I went to see my mother," Benny said, knowing that his lie would not fly. Sky then pulled out photos of Benny and Agent Shaw. Benny's face turned a beet-red color.

"You want to know how I got these?" Sky asked. "What did you tell them Benny?"

"They asked me about an agent and Mona. I told them that I didn't know what they were talking about. That's all, I swear," Benny said.

Sky looked at Benny and smiled. He then kicked him into the water and fired multiple shots into Benny's body. "Clean this up. Find out what you can on Agent Shaw," Sky said as he left the docks.

Second Chance

Four Months Later
Colima, Mexico
March 7, 2013
11:36 a.m.

Anisa and Rosita had grown close; thankful that Rosita had tended to her every need. There was no denying that Rosita saved Anisa's life. Although she was recovering, there was room for improvement. Anisa wore a piece of cloth that covered the left side of her face, but didn't have the nerve to look into a mirror since she had been left for death.

Anisa was running on a treadmill watching Mona's case on the television. Mona's situation was being covered by all of the major outlets. She had been denied bail, and the judge made it clear that he would not grant bail in the future. Mona was perceived as one of the most dangerous women in U.S. history. Forbes had estimated her criminal enterprise to be valued in the billions, making her the wealthiest woman in the United States.

Nobody knew that Anisa was alive and she wanted to keep it that way. Rosita knew Anisa had a dark side, but she didn't deserve to die. "She sounds like a bad woman," Rosita said as she walked into the room and saw what Anisa was watching. Anisa just smirked, thinking about all the things Mona had taught her. "Your gauze is heavy and needs to be changed," Rosita said. The dead tissue had to be scrapped from her body and treated with a medical solution. While the process was rigorous, Anisa could only think about getting well and the opportunity to release her rage. And Mona needed her now more than ever.

Anger and rage are a mixture of emotions that'll create a catastrophic disaster. We're all subjected to falling victim to circumstances. Ain't nobody exempt from that formality. We don't choose our fate or demise. Principles and morality are safeguarded by the legacy you leave behind. So, make a life worth living and a death worth memorializing…

***

Chicago, Illinois
March 9, 2013
9:39 p.m.

Yatta and his team were acquiring money and didn't know what to do with it. Yatta discussed the situation with Sky. With Mona out of the picture, Yatta would have to assume more responsibility in her organization. Yatta hoped for the best, knowing that the Feds had it in for Mona.

Capone asked Yatta to come by his house. He had something to show him. When Yatta entered the downstairs of Capone's house, he found a complete studio. Capone had spent one million dollars on the equipment, and had decided to invest in his own label. Now he had an artist he wanted Yatta to hear.

"What's this? You a rapper now?" Yatta joked.

"I'm about to start my own label. I want you to check something out," Capone said as he turned to the booth. He gave Rebel the signal to start rapping.

Moms say the devil lurk
Even preachers in the church
Wit a sermon full of scriptures
and a shovel full of dirt
Tryna bury imperfections and infection
in the church
See my own flesh and blood left me
hanging on a rope
Now these words unfamiliar feel'en
burning in my throat
tryna figure out this God shit
while holding on to hope
And this anger that's in me
it's embedded at the root
Hot headed like the copper
In a Ruger when it shoot

Rebel's maturity and the depth of his music's lyrical content impressed Yatta. While Rebel was only seventeen, his struggle was real. He had no mother and his father was doing life in prison. Rebel was raised on the streets and lived the gang culture. While hungry for a different path, he needed someone to show him the way.

Capone was all in on Rebel, ready to take him mainstream. "This is the man I was telling you about," Capone said as he introduced Yatta to Rebel.

"Yo, I heard a lot about you big homie. You're the engine that make the train go," Rebel said.

"Nawl, we're the train and it runs as a unit," Yatta said. Yatta stayed for a minute and talked with Capone and Rebel. He supported what Capone was doing for Rebel and applauded his efforts.

***

Williston, North Dakota
Women's Federal Holding Facility
March 11, 2013
8:19 a.m.

Mona was talking on a cell phone when the warden walked up. She stood up to face him. "Why do I get the feeling that we don't have an understanding?" Mona inquired.

"Mona, you're the most talked about woman in the country. You're being monitored and scrutinized by all of the wrong people to have hovering over you," Warden Hodges replied, hoping that Mona would understand.

"I put two million dollars into your pockets. Let's not have any misunderstandings. I'm not asking you for any favors. I own you," Mona was livid. Warden Hodges hadn't been allowing Mona to dominant his jail and Mona was pissed. She hated being locked up in the cell all day.

"You're going to arrange for me to see the governor, and if he doesn't agree, you convince him otherwise," Mona said. Two officers stopped and Mona gave them a set of instructions. "There's an officer that works second shift. Green, Lieutenant Greene. He's to have an accident leaving work," Mona instructed. The men agreed and left Mona to herself.

***

Juarez, Mexico
March 13, 2013
3:50 p.m.

Carlos and his Street General Hector Cuadras had made progress in their plans to control Mexico and eventually the United States drug trade. Mona's fall wasn't something that Carlos participated in, but he was ready to capitalize on her newfound misery. With Anisa dead and Mona locked away, now was the time to cripple her syndicate. Carlos would start by cutting off the drug pipeline. With no drugs to push, the underworld would have an opening for Carlos to close. Hector had proven himself, but it was still too early to know how reliable he would be. The war against the Cartels and the Mexican military was treacherous. While Carlos was influential in the Mexican underground, his goal was to unite all of the Cartels under one regime called the Laraza Cartel. Carlos had a vision of leaving his mark in the world before he expired. There was nothing left to stifle his objective. The Sheridan Syndicate would be destroyed.

Ambition creates nothing more than a man's will to succeed. You can't teach grit, it's something you must have instinctively…

A voice To Be Heard."

Chicago, Illinois
March 17, 2013
10:36 p.m.

This is my life
it's more than a story
just follow my lead
I lead you to Glory
I got what it take
I battled the odds
They pray to the lord
But I be the God
They praying to me
My pop in a cage
My Momma an addict
Addicted to crack
My life is the streets
Don't hustle or grind
then how we gone eat
I'm use to the struggle

the pain, the sorrow, the tussle
Embracing my troubles
My vision is blurred
Now I'm seeing double
help me indeed
Oh lord

Rebel was in the booth finishing a track for his latest album. Nobody had any idea that he was in the studio recording when they walked in. Key and Deno were listening as Capone smiled in approval of young Rebel's grind to make it with his musical endeavors. When Rebel walked out of the booth and saw everybody smiling, he froze.

"I ain't know ya'll was here," Rebel said.

"You sound like you going through it," Deno replied.

"Sometimes when I'm alone, the pain comes out. I vent better that way," Rebel shared.

"We here for you. You like family," Key assured him.

"Shit so crazy. Just last night my homie got killed," Rebel said. "I had decided to call it a night, had them drop me off and bro got in my seat. Ten minutes later, he got shot eight times. That would've been me. Yo, this music my outlet and it has to work. If not, I'm not going to make it off the streets alive." Rebel's passion could be felt through the struggle that came from his voice.

"Who going to tell my story if I'm not here?" Rebel added. Tears filled his eyes, leaving Capone with no choice but to hug him.

"We're on the journey to a better story to tell. Ain't no more dead homie stories to tell," Capone spoke with conviction. Yatta walked in and leaned against the door panel. Nobody knew he was there. He smiled at the close knitted circle of friends that called themselves family. Yatta hated how most people that come from urban society find the struggle to be part of life. This isn't supposed to be the story that most are forced to endure, but it is. He slowly disappeared up the stairs and left them to it.

Pain is real, just as the struggles keep one at a disadvantage…

***

Dallas, Texas
March 21, 2013
9:47 a.m.

Jasmine and Janice Lockhart were discussing Mona's current situation and the affect it could have on the company. Sky listened and understood their concerns. He assured them that Meddstone was a priority and Mona would put the safety of the company first. The Lockhart sisters were extreme loyalist and wished nothing but the best for Mona.

"The Panel Project is still a go and the funding is covered as previously discussed," Sky assured them. "Our company's lawyers are working on the contracts as we speak. The property we're focusing on is the Exxon property in the Pacific and Atlantic. That's our goal and we will achieve that – no exceptions!"

Sky knew Mona needed him to step up. Meddstone and the Royal Diamond Casino and Resort are a priority that he would guard with his life. These companies are beyond essential to their syndicate. And so is finding Ty.

***

Chicago, Illinois
March 24, 2013
11:16 p.m.

Yatta found his past to be a puzzle not easily understood. While Mona provided him with more questions, she allowed him to see that the things he thought were lies. He had to find Keyanna, his little sister. Perhaps she had some answers. With his personal life a mystery and Mona's falling apart, Yatta's path was challenging. He hadn't told anyone about the revelations that he discovered: Peter Rosenthal was his biological father, Nate was his brother, and Keyanna was his little sister.

The Missing Mother

Kingston Upon Hull, United Kingdom
April 1, 2013
9:03 a.m.

Agent Shaw rang the doorbell and waited. He had never seen a home so boastful in its appearance; massive and unimaginable with its castle-like structure. "How may I help you Sir?" a butler asked as he opened the door.

"Is this the residence of Ms. Loretta Williams?" Agent Shaw asked politely.

"Yes," the butler answered, welcoming Shaw into the lobby. Not to be outdone by the outside appearance, the interior was a mixture of marble, granite, glass and fine oak. Massive crystal chandeliers hung from high ceilings that seemingly reached to the sky. Spiral staircases ran throughout the two levels of the structure, and an elevator stood in the center of a mirrored wall.

"Wow," Agent Shaw thought as he stood in awe. The butler led him to a library where an elderly woman awaited his arrival. She had long platinum hair and hazel green eyes. She was an attractive older woman, appeared to be in good health, and was the mirror image of Mona.

"You've traveled quite the distance Agent Shaw. Finding me must have been a challenge," the woman said as she closed her book. She extended her hand and greeted Agent Shaw with a smile.

"Yes, the journey was long, but finding you was the biggest challenge," he admitted. I'm in no position to be modest and I mean not to intrude," Agent Shaw said.

"We're past that, but I can assure you that I'm of no use to you," Loretta said with an understanding as to why the agent was there.

"When was the last time you heard from your daughter?" Shaw asked.

"My daughter died a long time ago. Mona isn't my daughter. Latrice was not the person Mona is now. I never raised her to be the woman I despise today. And I haven't heard from her in twenty years, maybe longer," Loretta admitted. "Mona was my only child and our relationship is non-existent for as long as I can remember.

"You have quite the home. It must be very expensive," Shaw observed.

"Agent Shaw, don't come into my home to insult my integrity or patronize my values. I've worked for a good deal of my life and have acquired things without taking any short cuts," she snapped back, angered by his insinuation.

"I'm sorry Ms. Williams. Mona is a very dangerous woman and my job isn't just to put her away but to stop her. Locking Mona up won't put an end to her dealings."

"Agent Shaw, Mona is what you call an extreme intellect. She's gifted in terms of having the ability to think. When Mona was a child, she understood *Genetic Compounding.* At thirteen she decoded the atom and molecule research theories. She not only excelled in accomplishments, she did so effortlessly. Mona is a computer, a methodical tactician and a vindictive extremist."

"So what are you saying?" Agent Shaw inquired.

"You can't stop her by putting her in a cage. You can bury Mona in a bunker with thirty feet of steel and soundproof walls. It won't be enough," Loretta said.

"What are you suggesting?" Agent Shaw asked.

Loretta leaned forward and whispered as if Mona could hear her. "You better kill her because the moment she becomes bored being locked up, she'll find freedom beneath her feet."

"Mona's in a secured facility," Agent Shaw assured her.

Loretta laughed. "I don't think you understood a word I just explained. Mona's only in a jail cell because she likes the challenge of finding a way out. You don't get it. It's all an equation that she finds worth solving. And believe me, she will solve it."

***

Williston, North Dakota
Women's Federal Holding Facility
April 2, 2013
12:00 a.m.

While the meeting with the Governor didn't go as planned, she didn't allow that to deter her. She focused on Meddstone and The Royal Diamond Casino and Resort. Mona's attorneys worked overtime to make certain that every loophole was closed, leaving nothing to jeopardize her organization. She was not worried about her court circumstances. They would work themselves out.

"What are the chances of Ty and Sky staying out of the Feds sight? I know the Feds will use them to get to me." Mona asked Erin Crossfalls. The attorney was beyond loyal to Mona and had proven himself numerous times.

"At this point, nothing is certain. There's a mole inside your organization, and based on the things the Feds claim to know, it's somebody close."

"How did the meeting go with The Sheridan Corporation?" Mona asked.

"Everything is taken care of. No worries about that end," Erin Crossfalls assured her.

"Any word on Anisa?" Erin inquired.

"She'll surface. I'm sure of it," Mona answered. "I need you to contact her father and make sure the map I sent him is in a safe location." She stood and placed her hand on Erin's shoulder. "It's going to be alright. Trust me," Mona said to her good friend. He looked at her with a degree of uncertainty.

***

Colima, Mexico
April 6, 2013
9:00 p.m.

Anisa was undergoing the rigorous battle of taking herself off the heroin. Despite the withdrawals, her body was healing at a rapid pace. Anisa felt as if Rosita not only saved her life, but had given her the strength to start another one. While she wanted to pursue a new journey, there was something she had to finish before moving forward. Mona needed her and Anisa was pushing herself to get there. She had no idea as to what happened with Ty and that was only one of the troubles that stood before them.

Anisa was fond of the locals and familiar with the streets of Colima. She built a relationship with their neighbor, Bella, who helped with Anisa's care. Bella found Anisa to be an easy person to talk to, confiding that she ran drugs for the Mendoza Cartel. Any association with Mendoza hit Anisa with unimaginable anger, but Anisa didn't allow it to surface during their discussion.

Anisa learned that Bella inherited the debt that her father owed to the Cartel. He was a drug runner. He was directed to make a trip to the United States and bring back a van full of cash. But he never made it back. The

Cartel turned to his family to clear the debt. Usually, they would've killed the entire family. But Bella offered to run drugs in exchange for the safety of her mother and little sister.

"What Cartel do you work for?" Anisa asked again to assure herself that she was not mistaken.

"I work for Hector with The Mendoza Cartel."

"How do you get into the states?" Anisa continued prying for information.

"The Mendoza Cartel works with The Cuadras Cartel. They have tunnels that run under the border," Bella explained. Anisa listened intently.

"They have police and government workers on their pay roll. They pretty much run Mexico," Bella added.

"How do they pick people to run for them?" Anisa asked.

"Anybody can work. There's no official requirement. Ain't anybody crazy enough to miss with those people. As long as you're willing to take the risk, they'll allow you to run. Wait, Bella said. You're not thinking about running are you?" Bella asked.

"Maybe," Anisa replied.

"These people are dangerous and they won't hesitate to kill for the smallest of reasons. If my advice counts for anything, don't fool with these people," Bella explained with genuine concern.

"Anisa – bandage change, let's go," Rosita called out. She overheard the conversation between Bella and Anisa, and was concerned. "You making any plans that I need to know about?" Rosita asked.

"If you're trying to ask me something specific, just do it," Anisa replied.

Rosita looked into her eyes and saw nothing worth mentioning. All she saw was rage. "Did Bella tell you how the Cartels found her father and what they did to him? If she didn't, let me tell you. They cut out his tongue and did the same to his eyes. They then brought him back here and dismembered his body, hanging it on the street post like old shoes you throw over electrical wires," Rosita said while changing the bandages. She looked into Anisa's eyes and spoke, "Don't go get in bed with them people. You barely made it out of Juarez alive. I know the Cartels were responsible for what happened to you. For whatever reasons, I don't care. You got your life back, now live it. Once you're able to travel, I would get as for from this place as possible," Rosita said.

"I'm thankful for everything you've done for me, but there's a lot of things you don't know about me. I'll have to do some things in the near future that you'll find unbearable. I'm not leaving this world until I've finished what was started." Anisa was serious and Rosita knew it. She felt sorry for Anisa and knew there was nothing else to say.

Pain cuts deep, but not deeper than hatred...

"Sky Delivers A Message."

New York, N.Y.
April 10, 2013
1:36 p.m.

"Yo, I had the bitch in the spot last night and Niggaz thought I was going to set the hoe out right. So, I smashed and bounced. Keep in mind, we smoked all that weed and drank the bottles. Yo, them Niggaz was heated when I left with shorty." Jason fell out in laughter.

"You mad foul son – word." One of his homies joined in hunger. Jason and his home boys were hanging on the stoop, a black truck pulled up and parked.

"Who is that B?" Jason asked his crew, but neither of them had a clue. The men weren't strapped, but that didn't stop them from acting as if they were. Sky got out of the truck with a couple of men and approached Jason and his friends.

"You must be Jason," Sky said.

"What, you looking to hire me for something or…" Jason asked.

"Nothing of the sort," Sky cut him off. Jason saw how well dressed Sky was and assumed him to be a businessman.

"You're going to stay away from Marcella. The next time you put your hands on her, you don't want to know what happens next," Sky said.

"What, you threatening me?" Jason asked as he stood up. Two cars pulled up and seconds later a group of men walked up. Jason saw they were the Law that ran the spots. Jason worked for them. Everybody in New York respected Law and knew he wasn't the man you wanted problems with. Jason saw him and gained more courage than what he started with.

"You think shit sweet? Nigga, do you know where you at son?" Sky smiled at his antics.

"Sky, what's up homie? What's the problem?" Law said as he greeted his good friend and business associate. Sky supplied Law with guns and drugs. He even helped Law clean his money. Their relationship was solid and the two respected each other.

"Nawl, just giving Jason some advice. He likes to put his hands on women," Sky replied.

"You know who this is?" Law asked as Jason shook his head no.

"This like my brother. You piss him off. You piss me off. Whatever he told you, you hear that or we're going to have some problems. Word is bond," Law said, sending Jason on his way.

"You won't have a problem out of him. God – word is bond," Law said while walking Sky to his vehicle. "I see that shit with boss lady being highly advocated. If I can help, let me know," Law said with all intentions of doing so.

"I'll keep that in mind," replied Sky as he shook Law's hand and went about his way.

This is a small world, so be careful of the individuals you taunt. They may just know the people you dread…

***

Chicago, Illinois
April 13, 2013
10:32 p.m.

Capone and Rebel were in the studio working on his album. Rebel was ready to take the recording industry by storm and that was only the beginning. Capone listened as Rebel's lyrics blared through the speakers…

I was just a youngin still
so I learned the game for real
Moms in the kitchen wit me
lessons while the stove cooking
Blind to the streets
I had to hustle – I was still looking
witnessing the transactions
hand to hand coke deals
Poppi off the boat to flood the streets
You know the coke real
Clumsy in the house
I bumped the table -- caused the coke spill

When Rebel finished he walked from the booth. He had been working in the studio for twelve hours and was exhausted. That's what Capone liked about Rebel. He had the work ethic in addition to the talent.

"What you think about starting the video shoots?" Capone asked.

"Let's do it!" Rebel shouted.

"I'm going to make arrangements so we can get to that. I've got to make a run. Catch you tomorrow," Capone said as he left the studio.

***

Colima, Mexico
April 17, 2013
1:09 a.m.

Anisa was awaken by a woman's screams outside her window. The noise and rumbling sounds came from next door where Bella lived. Anisa ran downstairs, finding Rosita looking out the window blinds. Rosita's face was filled with worry as Anisa told her to turn out the lights.

"Those are Cartel members. They're going to hurt Bella," Rosita cried.

"Stay inside and lock the door behind me," Anisa said.

"What?" Rosita gave a confused reply.

"I said to lock the door behind me." As Anisa unlocked the screen gate, Rosita told her to wait. She went to her room and returned with a shotgun.

"This used to belong to my husband. Take it," Anisa obliged, skillfully checked the chamber and loaded it. She grabbed a knife from the kitchen and left the house. When she arrived at Bella's house, the back door was kicked in. Bella was screaming. A man stood at the stairs. Anisa slowly approached him and placed the barrel against his side. When he looked up, Anisa put her fingers against her lips, signaling him not to make a sound. She then removed a gun from his waistband.

"How many men are upstairs?" Anisa asked.

"Three, there's three," he replied with a shaky whisper.

Anisa told him to walk up the stairs. When he made it to the top of the stairs, Bella was being sexually assaulted. The abuser turned and saw the man standing at the top of the stairs. Anisa was concealed behind him and out of sight. "What the fuck, Jose? You supposed to be standing watch down stairs," the abuser said.

Jose didn't reply. "Hey stupid. You hear me talking to you?" The man snapped as he began walking towards Jose. When close enough, Anisa pulled the trigger, blowing a hole through one man and into the other. Anisa shot both men again and then took aim at the other two. She hit one and the other put a blade against Bella's neck.

"Bitch, we work for the Cuadras Cartel. You have no idea who you're fucking with. Put the gun down or I'll cut this bitch throat," he ordered. Anisa did as she was told and put her hands in the air. When the man went to pull his gun, Anisa swiftly took the knife from her waistband and threw it through the air and into his shoulder. As Bella ran, Anisa rolled forward, grabbing the shotgun in stride and shot the attacker. Anisa stood over him and fired off another round. Anisa wrapped a sheet around Bella. As the two walked down the stairs, another man met them. Just then, Rosita entered the house.

"Anisa, no. Please. Nobody else has to die. Put the gun down," Rosita pleaded.

"Yeah, put the gun down," the man said with a smirk to his face.

Boom!

Boom!

His body hit the ground. As Rosita began praying, Anisa grabbed her. "Your God won't help us right now. Go home and pack. We have to go. There will be more of them," Anisa said.

"Where would we go. I don't have nothing," Rosita said as tears raced down her face.

"We're going to the states," Anisa said and walked away.

"We Have An Agreement."

Bogota, Colombia
April 19, 2013
9:37 a.m.

Marcella's mother, Soria Sanchez, dominated the Colombia underworld. Soria was a shrewd businesswoman and a force to be reckoned with. Her father was a political leader in Colombia, a representative for their nation on the world stage. He endorsed his daughter's illicit endeavors and sheltered her from the governmental tactics aimed to dismantle her reign.

Sky arrived at the mansion and was met by armed guards. They escorted him to Soria's living area. Sky was uncertain how to approach her and his reason for being there. A few months ago, Soria paid Sky a visit at The Royal Diamond Casino and Resort. After they had discussed business, Soria mentioned that she was aware of Sky and Marcella's relationship, making this an awkward trip for him. But he was left with no other options.

"What's the pleasure of your trip?" Soria asked as she walked into the room.

"Business," Sky replied.

"I'm all ears," Soria answered.

"We had to cut ties with our old supplier. There's a void that needs to be filled and I don't have many sources to turn to," Sky explained.

"We already have an agreement. I operate on certain terms for a reason and never act outside of my comfort zone. I do what works for me," Soria replied. "I don't run a Cartel or any similar organization. I'm a businesswoman, nothing else."

Soria knew about Mona's situation and that her Syndicate was under the microscope, and didn't want any of Mona's heat to touch her. "That's understandable," Sky said, sounding a bit defeated. But Soria was loyal to Mona and wanted to help in anyway that did not jeopardize her situation.

"Let's talk numbers and product," Soria gave in.

"A thousand to two thousand kilo's a month," Sky said.

"Eight hundred, no exception and that's only for a span of eighteen months. This infringement on my supply line will cause me to make some adjustments. My word is my lifeline and I promised my people I wouldn't push that much product into the United States. I don't look to bring problems my way – just money."

"I can accept that and I appreciate your compromise," Sky said.

"We're all friends and Mona would do the same had I ever been in need of anything," Soria said.

"Thank you," Sky said with the deepest gratitude.

"No need for that. How is she doing?" Soria asked.

"Who?" Sky asked not realizing what she meant.

"Mona, not Marcella," Soria clarified.

"She's well, but her situation is uncertain," Sky said

"You'll get our shipment in a couple of weeks. Are you and Marcella serious?" Soria asked.

"Honestly, we're just friends and I care about her," Sky replied. Soria smiled and told Sky to watch where he stepped. While he didn't know what to make of her statement, he concluded their impromptu meeting and headed back to the states.

***

Juarez, Mexico
April 21, 2013
9:39 a.m.

Carlos blew a puff of smoke into the air and congratulated President Gomez for winning his second term.

"We have a good thing going here and this is only the beginning," President Gomez said. "What about the border?" Gomez added. "The United States can create a lot of problems with the construction of that wall."

Carlos knew the U.S. wanted to keep the Cartels out of their country, and building a wall was only the start of something he feared. "We can't fight that issue right now. I have to allow the federal government to do their job. If I intervene, it would draw some red flags and that would be a problem. Keep in mind that the United States and Mexico have a joint task force dealing with the issue," President Gomez explained.

"What about pulling the military out of Juarez?" Carlos asked.

"Juarez had more murders in a month than the middle east had in six. So, you answer that," President Gomez shot back.

"I guess you're right. I never looked at it that way," Carlos replied.

"The strong hold that the Cartels have in the country are bad. It's a war that leaves me with no other choice but to fight," the President answered.

"That's understandable Mr. President," Carlos commented.

Carlos was about to take Mexico by storm and there was nothing anybody could do. Once he was established throughout the entire country, he would turn his attention to the United States, and seize control of the underworld. War wasn't inevitable, it had already begun.

***

Fort Smith, Canada
April 26, 2013
11:19 a.m.

Agent Kemp found her new life more relaxing in Canada than back in the states. She believed the running was over, at least for now. Ty began to show more brain activity and his doctor said that was a good sign. As for the agency, she had no idea where to begin. She didn't trust anyone and for now, she was using her training to stay invisible.

"You sure know how to swing an axe," a man said to agent Kemp. She turned and faced a dark skinned man.

"It's the only thing my father ever taught me," Kemp replied. "I grew up in the woods and chopping wood came with the lifestyle," she lied. Kemp was missing her daughter and it hurt when erasing her from ever day thoughts. Kemp's training taught her how to cut herself off from the rest of the world and focus on the task at hand.

"Looks like he taught you well. My name is Jake. I just moved to the other side of the woods. I was doing some exploring and here I am."

"Nice meeting you," Agent Kemp said as she collected the firewood. When Agent Kemp was inside her home, she peered out the window. You can never be certain about anything.

"She's Back."

Miami, Florida
April 30, 2013
8:45 a.m.

Since Sky hadn't been by Mona's estate in some time, he decided to check out the property. When he opened the door, he smelled breakfast. Sky pulled out his gun and walked to the kitchen. He assumed there would be squatters inside and they were in for a rude awakening. But when he entered the kitchen, he couldn't believe his eyes. It was Anisa and some strange women. He immediately noticed how bad she had been injured and he cringed inside with anger. He walked up to Anisa and embraced her with a compassion one has for their best friends. "You're still a beautiful woman and I'm glad you're back. I need you," Sky admitted.

"Let's go somewhere and talk. We have a lot of catching up to do," Anisa replied as they left the kitchen. So much was going on and Mona remained incarcerated in a holding cell. In addition to Mona, the two of them had grave concerns for The Sheridan Syndicate and all of the things they worked so hard to accomplish.

***

Williston, North Dakota
Federal Court Building
May 1, 2013
9:30 a.m.

When Mona walked into the courtroom, there were newspaper reporters, media personnel, and a crowd of locals. Mona's charismatic smile and her self-assured poise earned their attention. Erin Crossfalls and his legal team were prepared to fight for Mona. Today they would be filing a motion for a change of venue. They believed that Judge Ryan Law wouldn't give her a fair trial. The judge's assessment of Mona was shown to be both prejudice and bias.

"Good morning. For the record, this matter is in regards to case number 13-CR-1901, Mona Moore vs. The United States of America." As Judge Ryan read the list of charges, Mona smiled. "Before I hear the defendants motion, I will address the mountain of acts vs. Moore. You have been charged with serious crimes – murder, conspiracy to commit murder, murder for hire, racketeering, embezzlement, money laundering, fraud, continuing a criminal enterprise, homeland terrorism, kidnapping, bribing a government official – I can keep going," the judge said, taking his glasses off and looking at Mona with disgust in his eyes. "These are mind boggling charges and the indictments are still coming in," the judge added.

"Your honor, we have no knowledge of any murder or related charges by way of indictments," Erin Crossfalls said as he cut the judge off.

"Well, now you do," the judge replied and advised the bailiff to hand the lawyer Mona's recent indictments.

"Ms. Moore, if these charges are accurate, so help you God. Anybody who endorses these acts are just as guilty as the person committing them, and they should be put away and punished to the full extent of the law," Judge Ryan said.

"Seems as if you have no taste for me, your honor. Quite bias to be frank. Shouldn't that alone be a conflict of interest to proceed before a judge that doesn't know how to separate his personal feelings from the job he's elected to do?" Mona mocked.

"I've been on the bench for nearly thirty years. My work speaks for itself," the judge replied.

"I see, like Senator Cullerton and Attorney General Law?" Mona knew about the corruption that the judge was tied to and she knew that this would strike a nerve.

"Your honor, please disregard my client's outburst. She's under duress due to her incarceration," Erin Crossfalls said in her defense.

Judge Ryan was livid. "I know who you are and what you do for a living. I'm not scared of you either. You will pay for your crimes if it's the last thing I do from the bench. You're a monster and don't deserve to walk the streets of America," the judge snapped.

Mona smiled and began to clap. "Did I strike a nerve your honor?" Mona inquired.

"Ms. Moore's motion for a change of venue has no merits and should not be validated," the judge snapped and banged the gavel.

***

Williston, North Dakota
Women's Federal Holding Facility
May 2 2013
8:00 a.m.

Agent Shaw sat across from Mona and studied her facial expressions. He looked for the monster that hid behind her natural beauty and soft-spoken words. "I heard you had an entertaining dialogue with Judge Ryan," Shaw said.

"Provoking, maybe. But entertaining, not even close," Mona replied with sarcasm.

"You do know that you're not getting out. You will die in prison," Agent Shaw said.

"That's where you're wrong. You'll die before me. In fact, you're going to die in a place like this," Mona promised. Agent Shaw found disgust in her words. "Do you know what lions do to their prey before devouring it?" Mona asked.

"Not really, but tell me." Shaw was curious.

"First the lion forces it's will and allows the prey to know it's being dominated and forced into despair. Then, death slowly consumes it." Mona was a woman with vision and not one to be taken lightly. Her focus was steady and precise and wasn't one to shy away from any challenge.

"I'm going to watch you fade away in prison. It will be my pleasure to see you twenty years from now clinging on to life," Agent Shaw said with a devious grin.

"You have no idea what kind of a ride you're in for. I'm not one to be dictated to," answered Mona.

"You think you'll get away with the things you've done?" Shaw asked.

"I guess we'll just have to wait and see won't we?" Mona shot back.

"Let me ask, you and the deceased Assistant Director, Cynthia Davis were childhood friends, correct?"

"Friends are always expandable," Mona answered.

"Why kill such a valuable asset? She must've decided she was tired of playing to your rules and wanted out?"

"I grow weary and tire of people who feel they have been granted titles of nobility," Mona said.

"So you did have her killed?" Shaw asked.

"You're asking all of the wrong questions," Mona said.

"When your trial begins, I'll get more than the answers I need. By the way, the prosecutor is seeking the death penalty," Shaw replied with a slight smile on his face.

"I can't wait," Mona replied with sheer arrogance.

Let your answers be stern and your actions be direct. But never assume that a ship cannot sink when it floats on a body of water…

Seek, Kill, And Destroy

Miami, Florida
May 3, 2013
11:16 a.m.

Anisa still had room for improvement, but her mobility had improved. She and Sky had a conversation about the things that had transpired throughout their absence, and how Sky found his greatest strength to be resilience. Anisa had the opportunity to speak with Mona and was overcome with emotions. Mona knew Anisa wasn't dead the moment she found out that her body wasn't recovered. Mona advised her that Red wasn't the informant. Now they were back at square one. Anisa knew the informant couldn't have been anyone outside of his or her immediate circle. But to think that information was being leaked from the inside wasn't something she wanted to put out there. So, Anisa would begin doing what she does best – seek, kill and destroy.

Mongo was out of the country focusing on tracking down Agent Kemp and Ty. Anisa needed him to handle a specific job but now it was a task she would have to tackle on her own. Anisa knew that Carlos would have to die and there was no exception about that, but for now she had to focus on the federal government and their endeavors to dismantle the syndicate. There was also a war to be fought with the Cuadras and that was something Anisa dreaded. Not out of fear, she just didn't have the time or patience. Mona's wellbeing comes first. Anisa was pressed for time and she knew the first person she needed to visit.

There was the annual Governor's dance that was hosted by Governor Perez. The event was intended to fund numerous charities that helped with land development and agriculture. Anisa walked in and blended into the crowd. Her face was covered with a partial lace cloth and matching sleeves to cover her burns. She was still beautiful, and from beneath the fire and ashes, she rose as an even stronger woman.

The venue was full of high-ranking government officials and inspiring political leaders. Anisa caught the eye of many noble, prestigious men ogling her with sexual intentions. She headed to the private room that held the guest of honor. Once inside, she grabbed a champagne flute and walked to the cigar section. Senator Cullerton saw her. The attorney general was there as well. Anisa leaned against the door panel and took a sip of her champagne. The senator was no stranger to Anisa and what she was capable of doing. Senator Cullerton walked her way, hoping not to cause a scene.

"Follow me," he said, and paused as he saw her "new look." When they made it to a private room, he closed the door. "How can I help you Anisa?" he asked.

"Whose the C.I. that's feeding information to the Feds?" she replied.

"You know I don't have access to that kind of information. That's above my clearance."

Anisa pulled a gun from her purse. "Luck hasn't been on my side as of lately, and time has been consuming. Let's not make this visit a bad one," Anisa threatened.

"I would have to call Judger Ryan. He's overseeing Mona's case. You want me to call him now?"

"Of course," Anisa replied. Senator Cullerton looked at Anisa for a moment, then proceeded to call Judge Ryan.

"Do you have any idea what time it is senator?" Judge Ryan asked.

"I'm sorry to disturb you but I have a problem and you're the only person that can help me."

"What can I do for you?" the judge asked.

"I need the name of the C.I. in the Mona Moore case."

"You know I can't discuss these things with you, especially not over the phone," the judge answered.

"How many favors have I done for you?" the Senator asked.

"You're putting me in an impossible situation. I'm sorry, but I can't discuss the Mona Moore case."

"Ryan, I practically put you on that bench. It's just a name for Christ sakes," the Senator spoke with a sense of urgency.

"Good night Senator, but allow me to ask you just one question. How did you know about there being a C.I.? That information hadn't been disclosed to anybody below." Senator Cullerton didn't reply as he hung up.

"I tried," the Senator said to Anisa.

"Sometimes that's all we can do," Anisa said, sending a bullet into his skull.

"The Mole Is Trapped."

Two Months Later…
District of Columbia
July 3, 2013
8:09 p.m.

Judge Ryan had concluded his day and was about to drive home. He made a detour to the men's room on his way out. After using the urinal, he walked to the sink to wash his hands.

"Judge Ryan, right?" A young man asked as he walked into the rest room.

"Yes, and you are?"

"That doesn't matter your honor," the man said as he locked the door. The judge headed for the door, but the younger man blocked him. Judge Ryan had seen enough cases play out in the courtroom to know that danger was inevitable.

"What is this about? I'm a federal judge son so you, you can get in some serious trouble."

"Mona sent you?" the judge asked.

"Some people you just don't fuck with," the younger man said.

"We can fix this," the judge pleaded.

"We're well pass that now aren't we?" The man said as he opened his suit jacket. He was wearing a suicide vest outlined with plastic explosives and too many ceramic ball bearings to count. The man said something in Arabic, then pushed the button.

At first nothing happened and then the roof exploded in a violent rage of heat and metal. The bomb leveled the entire floor and Judge Ryan died instantly. This was an act of war and Mona had declared it against the United States government.

War costs nothing but blood. Capital gain is just a bonus…

***

Miami, Florida
July 9, 2013
12:01 a.m.

Anisa learned that Mona had been shipped to a men's holding facility on the Army base in El Paso, Texas. She was the first woman in U.S. history to be held in a Supermax men's facility. Mona was an unofficial suspect in the bombing of a federal court building that left twenty people dead, including a federal judge. Although the evidence of Mona's involvement was circumstantial, they weren't taking any chances. She had the attention of all law enforcement up to and including the President of the United States.

"I think we should begin liquidating all of our assets. Mona's in a world of shit," Sky said. "This is getting out of hand."

"You do what you have to, but I'm not running. Mona needs me more than ever and I'll be here," Anisa shot back with all sincerity.

"Mona's on a suicide mission with this war against the government. She's my mother, but all of us can't make this sacrifice," Sky said.

"Like I said, you do what you have to do. I'm with Mona. If the ship goes down, then I'm going down with it." Sky looked at Anisa and then put his hands on his head.

"What's your plan?" Sky inquired.

"The head prosecutor has a high profile case in Chicago next week. According to my inside source, he has something on Mona that he hasn't shared with anyone. He's closed lip about it because he thinks Mona has somebody on the inside. So, he plans on using it when the trial starts," explained Anisa.

"That's a high risk job. Would your father help?" Sky asked.

"I don't want him to have his hands in this. I'm meeting with Yatta and we'll go from there," Anisa replied.

"You think Yatta will be on board?" Sky asked.

"I'm certain," Anisa answered with confidence as she walked out of the room.

***

Fort Smith, Canada
July 12, 2013
11:19 p.m.

Agent Kemp woke up to a loud bang. Her ears began to ring as she reacted the way she had been trained: Strap yourself into a bulletproof vest and grab your weapons. She knew this was a fight and she was tired of running.

Psst!

Psst!

Psst!

Kemp burned the barrel that hosted the silencer attached to it. She ducked as additional bullets drove her to the other side of the wooden barrier. These shooters were professionals.

Boom!

Boom!

Agent Kemp returned fire.

Psst!

Psst!

Psst! Psst!

Psst! Psst! Psst!

Agent Kemp was bombarded with an array of fire. She managed to make her way next to Ty' room. She would protect him no matter what. As long as she kept her assailants from making it upstairs, she had a chance. Kemp retrieved the shotgun from the closet and stuck the handgun in the small of her back. A flash bang had been tossed upstairs. Kemp ducked.

Boom!

She was momentarily disoriented while she regained her composure. Kemp was now in Ty's room. She pushed the dresser in front of the door and moved Ty's bed closer to the wall. Kemp looked out the window and saw two black SUVs. She was running out of time. Kemp had no other option but to do what she had to do. Time was of the essence and her life was hanging in the balance…

***

Chicago, Illinois
July 12, 2013
11:22 p.m.

Anisa contacted Yatta to take out the prosecutor, Ricky Hughes, and was assured that Yatta's team could handle the assignment. Anisa provided the routes and time to make the hit. The plan was underway.

Key raced her bike down the back streets and crossed onto the main road. A white town car was stopped at a light with a security detail behind it. Key jumped a lane and opened fire on the town car. She slammed on her brakes and spun the bike around. The town car was blocked in. The security detail's doors opened and several agents returned fire. Key got off her bike and engaged in combat. Ricky Hughes' car then pulled off during the distraction the moment it found a path. When Ricky's driver made it around the corner and a half block from the security detail, a van came out of the alley and smashed into the side of the white town car.

As the car spun out of control, two motorcycles appeared as Deno stepped out of the van. Yatta and Capone got off their bikes and opened fire on the white town car. Somehow the driver managed to bring the town car under control and began to pull away. "Shit!" Yatta yelled. They had a block to finish the job or all would be in vain. The car was getting away.

***

Fort Smith, Canada
July 12, 2013
11:50 p.m.

Agent Kemp fired through the door the moment she heard footsteps coming upstairs. Shots followed as she rolled out of harms way. Chaos everywhere. A flurry of shots riddled the door. Debris and shredded material polluted the air.

Boom!

Boom!

Boom!

Boom! Click. Click

The shotgun was empty. Agent Kemp threw it to the ground and pulled the handgun from the small of her back. Things grew quiet. Agent Kemp pulled out her phone.

“This is Agent Kemp, my tracker is now activated. Again this is Agent Kemp. She froze by what she just saw. Ty was awake. The two of them starred at each other. A small bang ensured and the door to the room had been destroyed. A group of men stormed the room and there was no fight left in Agent Kemp. Ty was awake as Kemp was making her distress call. The assailants surrounded her. Agent Kemp was struck over the head; darkness followed.

***

Chicago, Illinois
July 12, 2013
11:52 p.m.

“Drive… Drive…” Ricky yelled as he ducked in the back seat. The driver made a hard left, causing the car to roll. Capone stopped his bike near the white town car. The security detail came flying around the corner. Capone shot as he backed up. Key came hard from the alley and returned fire. Men in the detail shot at Capone’s fleeing motorcycle.

Yatta made his way around a parked van and found his target. Police sirens could be heard closing in. Yatta approached the white town car, saw his target, and pulled on the car handle. A policeman saw Yatta and opened fire. Yatta ducked for cover as Key and Deno fired at the policeman.

Capone pulled Yatta to his feet. “We have to go,” Capone yelled. Key and Deno were pinned down by gunfire as more policemen stormed the scene. Key tried to join Yatta, but a bullet ripped through her leg. Deno then helped Key to her feet.

“Y’all have to get out of here. We’ll cover y’all,” Deno yelled to Yatta.

“We’re not leaving,” Yatta replied. Capone looked at his brother as tears filled his eyes.

"I can't leave you bro," Capone said. Deno and Key knew somebody had to live and they were willing to sacrifice themselves. Key and Deno ran in the opposite direction of Yatta and Capon and fired multiple shots. While Yatta and Capone raced down the alley, Key was hit again. Deno stopped and grabbed her hand. A bullet caught the back of Deno's head. Key saw his eyes roll to the back of his head. He was dead. Key moved closer to the prosecutor, and fired off a few shots before feeling the pain of hot metal pull her under.

"My Brother Is Down."

Chicago, Illinois
July 12, 2013
12:15 p.m.

Yatta and Capone barely escaped with their life. Yatta turned on the television the moment they walked into their house. The news media was reporting the shoot out and attempted murder of federal prosecutor Ricky Hughes. He was shot twice and listed in critical condition. Deno had been fatally wounded and Key was in the hospital undergoing treatment for her injuries.

Capone took the news hard. Deno was his best friend and brother and the only living relative he loved. Deno sacrificed his life for them. All Yatta could do was hug Capone. Yatta felt responsible. He brought them into the job. So much had transpired since his release from prison and it wasn't all good.

Capone pulled away from Yatta and grabbed his gun. "That mother fuckers got to go. Bro and Key sacrificed themselves and he's not dead, so I'm gonna finish it," Capone snapped.

"You're not thinking straight," Yatta said. "You think you could just waltz up in a hospital and shoot a federal fucking prosecutor and walk out?"

"I don't care," Capone said, trying to push pass him. Yatta knew what he had to do. He grabbed Capone around the neck in a sleep hold and began to squeeze. Capone pulled and clawed until sleep tamed his violence. Yatta placed him on the couch to sleep off his rage. Key was fighting for her life and Deno was dead. The blood of his shadow had spilled.

Hatred suffers when anger can't rage, and it boils in grief beyond that of any other painful experience…

***

El Paso, Texas
Fort Dell Army Base
Federal Holding Facility for Men
July 19, 2013
9:39 a.m.

Agent Bristle sat across the table from Mona who held a slight grin on her face. They all knew that Mona was behind the bombing of the federal courthouse that killed a judge. And they also knew that it was her call that nearly killed Ricky Hughes. "You didn't succeed. Ricky Hughes is still alive," Agent Bristle said.

"For how long?" Mona played along.

"You think this is some kind of game don't you? You're not getting away with this and you will get the death penalty," Bristle said.

"Do you know what a lion does to his prey before eating it? Let me tell you. He forces his will and gives its prey the opportunity to feel its dominance. Then he kills it"

"Good thing you're no lion."

"Oh, I'm much worse."

"Really?"

"You think this Army base can hold me?"

"You tell me. You're on a fucking United States Army base."

"I guess we'll just have to see."

"Well, I have a lunch date and some fresh air to take in. Prisons aren't a place for me. You can die slow and have a nice day." With that, Agent Bristle left the room.

***

Chicago, Illinois
University of Illinois Hospital
Trauma Unit
July 20, 2013
8:17 p.m.

Key was to be escorted to a holding facility now that her wounds had been treated.

Ricky Hughes was still in bad shape, but a full recovery was expected. Key noticed that the policeman standing watch over her was sleeping. She dislocated her thumb and pulled out of the handcuffs. Once her feet touched the floor, she was a bit light headed. After regaining her equilibrium, she inched her way to the door. As she reached for the officer's gun, a nurse screamed, waking the officer. Key took his weapon and fired.

Boom!

Boom!

She then pointed the gun at the nurse. "Where's the prosecutor?"

"Room 142," the nurse answered.

Key headed to the room as the nurse ran away. Officers were racing to where they heard the shots. Key entered Ricky's room and locked the door. He was under heavy medication and had no idea he would never wake from his deep sleep. Key raised her gun.

Boom!

A shot came through the door and ripped through her shoulder. Key fired back as the door was kicked open. Key fired at the prosecutor as the officers rushed into the room.

Boom!

Boom!

Both shots found their mark and Ricky Hughes was dead.

When all else fails, my shadow don't…

"Attack On The Mexican Border."

Nogales, Mexico
Mexican Boarder/U.S. Crossing Center
July 23, 2013
2:30 p.m.

The United States and the Mexican Governments had a joint task force called the Anti-Cartel Neutralization Team (ANT). They fought in the trenches of Mexico's most dangerous cities that were overrun by the drug cartels. The Cuadras and the Mendoza Cartels had a strong hold on Mexico and operated throughout South America. The Mexico border and the United States crossing had captured nearly one billion dollars in contraband and two hundred million in cash over the past year. While the war against the Cartels was costly in terms of lives and manpower, it was necessary.

"Pull over," a border patrol officer ordered the occupant of a white van. An order had been sent down the chain of command to increase vehicle searches. When there's an increase in the consumption of narcotics on the streets of the U.S., the Cartels increase the supply of drugs pushed over the border and other alternative means. When the officers walked up to the van, they found a visibly nervous woman sweating profusely.

"Can you pop the back of the van?" An officer asked. The woman didn't respond.

"Ma'am, can you please open the back of your van for border inspection?" Another officer asked. When she didn't comply, they physically removed her from the van and began their search. One of the officers found a suspicious wire running from the dashboard to the back of the van. The wires led to a massive cooler wrapped with an unknown material. The officer backed up as he turned to his coworker.

"Get the bomb squad, now!" he said and turned to the woman who had tears running down her face.

"I'm sorry, they have my family," the woman spoke as she pushed some numbers into her phone. The van shook. A ball of flames engulfed it. Total chaos followed as sharp metal and bolts shot through the air like bullets. The doors of two large-sized buses opened, numerous men and women jumped out of the bus carrying duffel bags filled with drugs. Before order was restored, smugglers carried the duffel bags as they ran through the checkpoints and into the United States.

Drugs and violence go hand and hand. Money is only the bridge used to bring them together…

***

Hermosillo, Mexico
Border Recruitment Center
Emergency Response Unit
Same Day
3:00 p.m.

A border patrol officer stormed into the Commander Center petrified. "Help! They're coming."

Boom!

A Rocket Propelled Grenade (RPG) crashed into the entrance and exploded. A large number of officers had been dispatched to the U.S. Crossing and Mexican border to offer support to the officers under attack. Only a small number of officers were left behind. Numerous men from the Cartels stormed the entrance of the Border Recruitment Center and opened fire on the officers struggling from the effects of the exploding RPGs. A truck smashed into the back of the building and more assailants stormed the place totting AK-47s.

The remaining border officers radioed for help, but there was a frequency jammer that kept the message from being transmitted. The officers remaining alive were placed on the ground and forced to strip.

"My name is General Hector and I work for the Cuadras Cartel. We're hiring, who wants a job? The Sargent outside said this was a recruitment center. So, here I am. Anyone want a job?" Hector said. When no one replied, Hector shot one of the men in the head.

"Last offer," he said. Two men raised their hands. Hector gave them guns and told them to kill the remaining officers on the ground. Both recruited men killed their co-workers and headed out. Carlos was determined to take control of the drug trade in South America and this was just the beginning.

***

Chicago, Illinois
August 1, 2013
12:01 p.m.

Some people smile in order to hide the pain that boils beneath the surface. There's a point when all your patience has been exhausted and the hell that you thought was beneath the surface is hovering directly over you.

Yatta sat up in his bed and placed his hands over his face. He couldn't sleep and there was so much going on. His world had been turned upside down and whirling out of control. His heart was heavy with grief. Capone was lost within himself and the ground beneath him was crumbing. Yatta gave his comrade all the space he needed to mourn the loss of his brother and fallen shadow.

Key was in the county jail. It was too risky to contact her. Only time would tell if Yatta and Capone were considered suspects in the attack on the federal prosecutor. Yatta was not concerned about Key's loyalty, but confinement has a way of convincing one to act out of character.

Anisa offered all the help possible but Yatta assured her that Key would be taken care of. But what can Yatta do? Key had killed a federal prosecutor. Yatta had no idea what his future held. He had major drama in his personal life and Mona had a feud brewing with the government. Yatta needed to make a decision: fight or flight.

Sometimes mixing the sweet with the sour works but keep in mind that sugar does turn into shit...

Welcome Back

Sandpoint, Idaho
August 3, 2013
9:46 a.m.

Ty was receiving excellent medical care and while he was expected to have a full recovery, it would require some time. Anisa and Sky were staring at him when he opened his eyes.

"You good bro?" Sky asked. Ty tried to respond but his voice cracked. After a few attempts he found his words.

"How long was I out?"

"You were out for a while. Good to have you back with us," Anisa replied. Sky helped Ty sat up.

"Where's Mona?"

"She's out," Anisa said. They didn't want to worry him about her situation.

"What happened to you?" He asked Anisa as he noticed the burns on her body.

"I had an accident. I'm fine," she assured him.

Memories began surfacing while they talked; the shooting at the boat company; the flash of the muzzle; the shootout between Agent Kemp and

Mongo's team; the revelation that Agent Kemp was known to Ty as Olivia; and the strangest thing of all was the fact that Ty recalled every conversation Agent Kemp had with him while he was in a coma. For some reason, Olivia's words formed the pathway back to his consciousness.

"Where is she?" Ty wanted to know.

"Let us deal with her," Sky said while he noticed a darkness in his brother's eyes that he had never seen before.

"I'm not asking you to tell me where she is. Where the fuck is she?" Ty demanded.

"I'll take you to her," Anisa said as she called Mongo.

***

Mexico City, Mexico
August 4, 2013
9:29 a.m.

President Gomez walked into his presidential suite and took a seat on the sofa. He'd been busy with his political cleanup of the recent attacks on the border of Mexico. Dealing with his people was bad enough but the U.S. was a different animal. Mexico had a war raging out of control and he was smack dead in the middle of it.

"Mr. President, you have a visitor downstairs. He says it's urgent," one of the security guards said. The President knew exactly who it was.

"Send him up." He exhaled a puff of air in frustration. Carlos wasted no time expressing his distaste for Gomez's disappearance.

"You haven't been answering my calls. I feel as if you've been avoiding me," Carlos said.

"Maybe you should of thought about that before you decided to kill an entire platoon of border agents. Now guess who has the noble privilege of cleaning this shit up?"

"You need to watch who you're talking to. Keep in mind that I'm the reason you were re-elected. You signed up for this. Now you're going to do what's required to get things under control. Then you're going to pardon Juan Mendala Rodriguez," Carlos demanded.

"You have to be joking, right? Juan killed a high ranking government official – No way!"

"Estoy no es un pregunta! You'll make sure he's released," Carlos demanded. "te oldidas familia premero – I'll see you soon."

"What if I can't get it done?"

"You're a smart man Mr. President, let's not act otherwise." With that, Carlos left the room.

***

Augusta, Maine
August 5, 2013
11:17 a.m.

Her eyes reeked of deception and lies of convincing tales. Ty was filled with anger, betrayal and pain.

"Agent Kemp, right?" He inquired with sarcasm. She had been beaten badly by Mongo for information that she might have given to the Feds.

"Ty please, they're going to kill me."

"Not my problem," he said. "Your job was to deceive me and infiltrate my family and cause us harm. Bravo!"

"They don't have anything on you. The job was all about Mona. I swear."

"You do realize that she's my mother, the woman who brought me into this world; provided me with a lifestyle that only a small percent of people could ever experience? Is your name Olivia or is it a part of your cover?" Ty looked square into her eyes as he spoke.

"I'm a fugitive because I went against command and refused to turn you in. I took care of you and did right by you. I kept you alive and well."

"You should've killed me," Ty replied.

"So what now?" Agent Kemp asked.

"Maybe I should toy with you like you did with me, or just turn you over to Anisa. You've done enough digging into my families operation to know her angles and taste for traders, let alone Feds. Was anything about you true?"

"Yes! Everything wasn't about the job. You were just a means to get in. But I fell for you."

"Don't you fucking go there – don't," Ty said as he cut her off and stood up.

"It's true," Agent Kemp said as tears raced down her face. Ty was torn, but he had to choose the stability and loyalty that grounded his morals and dignity to his family. He loved her just as much as he loved his family, but loyalty trumps all. At least it should. What was the right decision? Follow his heart or stand by his family? Ty looked at Agent Kemp and chose his family.

"You chose your side, now I'm choosing mine."

"A Hit Man Is Freed."

Chicago, Illinois
August 9, 2013
1:19 p.m.

"I got you. We're all we got," Keyanna told Key.

"I never doubted you and I never will," Key replied.

"So what's our next move?" Keyanna asked.

"Yatta needs me. I'll figure something out," Key promised.

"I trust that you will. You got to get out of hear," Keyanna replied.

"I will, trust me," Key said as a guard approached.

"Who are you talking to Brown?" the guard asked.

"Nobody!" Key replied and smiled at the reflection in the mirror.

***

Villahermosa, Mexico
August 10, 2013
9:00 a.m.

Juan Mendala Rodriguez walked through the prison gates a free man. As he stopped and took a final look, he promised himself that he would die before returning. Fifteen years was a long time to be isolated from society. Juan was a hit man that belonged to no organization, but he felt close to the Mexican mafia. His loyalty was with Carlos for rescuing him from a life sentence. When Juan experienced his first glimpse of freedom, Carlos was waiting for him.

"Bienbenido a la casa her mano," Carlos said as he embraced his familia."

"Ase Mucho tienpo," replied Juan.

"Familia primero y para siempre – family always," Carlos assured him.

"Let's get out of here before someone above changes their mind and shackles you back down. We have so much catching up to do. First, let's welcome you home in style." Carlos opened the car door. Two beautiful women clad in nothing but jewelry were waiting for Juan.

Prison does nothing for a man, but teach him how to deal with solitude or be consumed by it. The incarceration is the cave that affects your mind, in which your mental state will become sucked into self-entangled bondage. Your mind is the prison, where your thoughts become the warden's and your actions are compelled by guard-like tenancies...

***

To be continued…

Preview from *"Blood of My Shadow: The Rise & Fall of the Syndicate"*

Book 2

by Jovon Scott

edited by Larry L. Franklin

Prologue

Guns were popping and cracking like fireworks on the fourth of July. Blood spilled onto the streets of Chicago. While some died, others were hauled to the nearest hospital; the place where bullet-ridden bodies are stitched back together, readied for another day. It had been two months since the fatal shooting. Yatta's team – Deno, Capone, Key, and himself – prepared to ambush federal prosecutor Ricky Hughes and his entourage of police officers. According to an inside source, Hughes had damaging information on Mona Moore's criminal case that he hadn't shared with anyone. He needed to be stopped.

The failed ambush left a handful of police dead and a severely injured Ricky Hughes. The attackers suffered loses as well – Deno was killed and Key had multiple gunshot wounds. Deno and Key had made the ultimate sacrifice so Yatta and Capone could escape.

Key and Hughes were transported to the Cook County trauma unit in Chicago, Illinois. It was there where Key regained consciousness, slipped out of her handcuffs, disarmed the officer assigned to her room and located prosecutor Hughes. She shot two bullets into his head before being taken to the floor by police officers. She was treated in the trauma unit and sent to a Chicago jail. Ricky Hughes was dead.

The governor called for the perpetrators to be penalized to the full extent of the law. Although Mona Moore was being held in police custody and unable to physically participate in the shooting, the entire state of Illinois believed that she was behind the attack. Yatta was left to suffer the emotional loss of his comrades; and for Capone, the death of Deno, his brother and best friend was beyond comprehension. Deno's *penumbra* -- his shadow -- was dead, leaving him with the *"Blood of my Shadow."*

Mona had multiple indictments including money laundering, racketeering, murder for hire, treason, and other criminal charges. She was also being investigated for the bombing of a federal building that left numerous people dead, including the federal judge assigned to her case. The United States and all of its law enforcement agencies were on full alert, ready to take any course of action deemed necessary. Mona had been transferred to an Army base to await trial.

Mona's absence from the Syndicate was causing rifts within the organization. Her sons, Ty and Sky, weren't in agreement with the standings of the companies and the pipelines used to distribute drugs throughout the United States. Anisa was trying to preserve the Sheridan Syndicate that Mona had established during her reign.

Losers and winners account for the atrocities acquired from the strides taken to gain success in their endeavors. But the first to recover from the conflicts endured in war, are favored to overcome the hostile encounter…

"My Brother Is Gone."

The Funeral…

A dark cloud loomed above the church as people paid their final respects to Deno. Capone's brother was taken from him; his *penumbra* was gone. Capone had not seen these people in several years; reminding him of an old saying – "*when the lights come on, the stars come out.*" Yatta, on the other hand, was trapped in the realms of perplexity as the reality of his losses refused to take hold. Since Yatta's release from prison, his life turned sour and tragedy found a home at his doorstep. He felt responsible for what had transpired, but realized his self-imposed blame would not alter the fact that Deno was dead and Key was locked up.

Capone sat in a church pew, watching people take the podium and share their memories of Deno. Capone stewed in his belief that the speakers pretended to care for his brother.

Yatta watched Capone down his drink and walk to the podium where he grabbed the microphone from a man paying his respects. "Hilarious, you people are so fucking funny," Capone said as he pulled a pint of *Remy* from his back pocket and took a couple of drinks; he had been drinking since his brother's death three days earlier. Yatta knew that nothing good would come from Capone speaking at the podium. But Deno was his brother. Who could tell Capone how to grieve?

"All of you people come here and act as if you really care. But where were you when Deno needed you the most?" Capone snapped. He slammed the bottle against the podium so hard that the glass shattered. Yatta rushed to remove Capone from the podium. Capone pushed him away, pulled a gun from the small of his back and fired into the air. "Everybody sit the fuck down. If you leave before I'm done paying my respects, I'll shooting until I run out of bullets." Everyone returned to their seats and saw the rage in Deno's eyes; a visual warning that he was prepared to kill.

Capone gathered himself and wiped the tears from his eyes. "Despite what others might think, my brother was a good man. He had my back even in the darkest moments. But I let him down..."

Yatta interrupted. "Capone, I know what you're going through. He was my brother too. This is not the way for him to be remembered. Give me the gun."

Capone saw a few people looking to slip out of the church. "If you leave the pew I will begin shooting." Capone continued. "Most of you don't know that Deno had a degree in business. Hell, he was the reason I went to college. He knew that one day we would need to find a way off the streets. I let him down and now he's dead."

Capone looked at the ceiling as if he was conversing with Deno. "I let you down bro. Now you're all alone." Capone took a deep breath, wiped his faced and looked at Yatta. "Shadows, right?" Capone asked.

"Yeah," Yatta answered. "You already know."

Capone placed the gun against his head. Yatta reached for the gun but was too late. Capone pulled the trigger. His body fell to the floor. People began running from the church while others seemed paralyzed as they watched Capone's body twitch.

Yatta punched the podium so hard that he shattered the bones in his hand. He didn't want Capone to go out like this. Now he was about to mourn the death of two brothers.

When a soul is consumed by grief and troubled with despair and there's no solace, perhaps the only act of compassion is death…

"A Split Between Brothers."

Juneau, Canada
September 4, 2013
9:19 a.m.

Twenty-five is not the ideal age to lead a multi-billion dollar criminal organization. But Ty and Sky were left to shoulder the leadership position of The Sheridan Syndicate while their mother, Mona Moore, was incarcerated. Due to a recent near-death attack by the Cuadras Cartel, doctors had placed Ty in a medically induced coma. Olivia, who had been Ty's personal assistant for the past five years, was nursing Ty back to health.

Olivia, a.k.a. Agent Kemp, was discovered to be an undercover agent working for the C.I.A., and recognized by the agency as the first agent to have successfully infiltrated the Sheridan Syndicate. What went unknown was the fact that Agent Kemp had fallen in love with her mark – Ty Moore.

Anisa was following an inside tip from the assistant director of the C.I.A. that a mole had infiltrated the Syndicate. Agent Kemp's cover was blown. To complicate matters, Kemp discovered that Mona Moore had ties within the C.I.A., leaving it unclear as to who she could trust. Kemp cut all communications with the C.I.A. and the outside world. She loaded Ty and his medical equipment, and together they headed for an isolated cabin in the mountains of northern Canada.

The Syndicate and the C.I.A. were on the prowl for Agent Kemp. Mona had sent for Mongo, a man from South Africa, who specialized in tracking people. In time, Mongo located Agent Kemp and Ty, and after a brief shootout, delivered them to Mona Moore. Kemp was unhurt. Ty had awakened from his coma and was improving faster than anticipated.

Members of the Syndicate were called in to discuss events recently transpired with the federal government and the continuous feud with the Cuadras and Mendoza Cartels. "I think we should kill the distribution line and hold off on pushing any product," Ty said. "With the feds breathing down our necks, I think we should focus on our legal activities until this blows over."

"I'm not in favor of your recommendation," Sky said. "There are too many moving parts. We have an entire network that will suffer if we do a complete shut down. Of course we should be cautious, but there's too much at stake to walk away. Keep in mind that we have a war going on. Killing our pipelines would leave our networks vulnerable, an opening that the Cuadras Cartel will exploit."

The disagreement between the brothers was obvious. "Our top priorities should be Meddstone Drilling and the Royal Diamond Casino and Resort. They produce a bulk of our revenue and provide an outlet to launder a shit load of capital," Ty added.

"I'm against anything that compromises our financial stability," Sky stated. "Shutting down the networks would piss off a lot of people, and more importantly, our supplier would have to unload their shipment." It was unusual to see the twin brothers on different sides of an issue. "You haven't been here for months," Sky added. You were in a coma. I've built this network to operate at a certain capacity and reworked our agreements with the supplier."

Sky felt empowered by the extended role he was forced to shoulder while Ty was absent, and was not ready to relinquish the power and control he had acquired. Ty allowed his brother to vent, knowing that at some point they were going to have a problem. Mona always understood how invigorating power and control can be, insisting that balance between members be maintained throughout the organization. Each member had a specific role to play and knew not to cross into the duties of others.

As head of the Shultz family, Anisa's vote within the Syndicate had become more important than ever. Her vote could be perceived as choosing one brother over the other, and could determine the future path of the organization. The Arturo family had been given a pardon from the table, allowing them to mourn the loss of Vino. Yatta and his family were emotionally devastated from their losses and were absent. The Lockhart sisters were business associates and not allowed to vote on Syndicate matters.

"Just so we're clear on what's going on, Mona's been accused of blowing up the fucking federal building, killing a number of civilians and a federal judge," Ty said as his voice began to crack. "This is beyond problematic. You do what you feel is necessary, but I will get out of your way before this train crashes and burns," Ty added.

"While I see valid points on both sides, closing down the network could cause a panic that we don't need at this time," Anisa said. "Other solutions will have to be found to accommodate the narrative concerning the feds."

"There's no need for accommodations," Ty said. "I'll do whatever is required of me. Let's see how things play out."

"From what our attorney, Mr. Crossfalls, has conveyed to me, the feds don't have anything that calls for an immediate raid. We weather the storm and move forward." Sky wasn't intimidated by the feds and wasn't going to stop what he had in place.

"Do you understand what's going on?" Ty asked. "Apparently you don't. We're not talking about being investigated by a local police department.

We're talking about the federal government. Any and all actions that'll cause unwanted attention should be taken off the table." Ty was losing his patience. "Keep in mind that Mona just declared war against the government with the bombing of the court house," Ty added.

Sky's anger surfaced. "You should be the last person to come here and talk about making rational decisions. You're responsible for bringing that fed bitch into our organization. And you're still holding her hostage," Sky ranted.

"Wait," Anisa yelled. "You mean to tell me that Agent Kemp is still alive, as in not dead!"

"Killing her now would leave us in the dark," Ty said. "We have no idea what she told the feds."

Anisa laughed in disgust. "As long as she is alive, she is a liability. Where is she?" Anisa wasn't in a humorous mood.

"She's in a safe place," Ty said.

"Maybe I wasn't clear," Anisa responded. "I'm not asking you to tell me where she is. I'm telling you." The look in Anisa's eyes was menacing.

"I don't answer to you. You work for me," Ty answered.

"That's where you're wrong," Anisa said. "I work for Mona's best interest and this organization. If anyone poses a threat, I'm authorized to eliminate them, and that includes you." Anisa stepped from her seat and headed to the helicopter. She was going to search every home Ty owned for a person who should be dead.

***

Augusta, Maine
September 5, 2013
11:51 p.m.

Ty walked into the house where Agent Kemp was being held and heard her screaming in excruciating pain. Mongo had been torturing her for the past six hours and was unable to break her. She was suspended from the ceiling by her arms and badly beaten. Her eyes were swollen shut, and she appeared to be near death.

Mongo stopped as Ty walked into the room. "I've been in this business a long time and I've broken the best," Mongo said. "There's no way that she knows anything that she hasn't told me. As Mongo picked up a hammer and was about to bash her head in, his phone rang.

"Hello… Sure I'm with her right now… Augusta, Maine at the house on 24th and Old Mills… I'll get right on it." Mongo ended the call and turned to Ty.

"That's an interesting call," Mongo said. "For some reason Anisa is under the impression that this woman should have been dead a long time ago. But you advised me that information needed to be extracted." Mongo was pissed and felt as if Ty had used him. Mongo then turned and raised the hammer to take a swing at Agent Kemp. Ty drew his weapon and fired a couple of rounds into Mongo's back. Mongo rolled over and faced Ty. He started to speak but was never given the chance. Ty shot him in the head.

Ty untied Kemp from the ceiling and checked her pulse. Only a hint of any pulse was felt. Ty looked at this unconscious woman as if he didn't know her at all, and had no idea why he was helping her. After all, she was an enemy of the Syndicate. Ty was pacing back and forth, and Anisa was on her way. Keeping Kemp alive was dangerous but killing her wasn't an option for Ty. He needed answers from her. She had deceived him in ways that were devastating.

Ty wrapped her naked body in a sheet and carried her out to his car. She needed help or she would die. Ty knew where he could take her. Once they were in his car, Ty made telephone calls to have the house cleaned and Mongo's body disposed of. So many things were running through his head and only Kemp had the answers. She knew things that could have incriminated him. Why didn't she act on them? He had no idea. For now, Ty had to convince Anisa that Kemp was dead and that he was back on track with the family. He called Anisa. "I just spoke with Mongo. It's done," Ty said.

"That's good to know, but I'm enroute to check for myself," Anisa replied.

"I already had the clean up, but I'll forward pictures once I land," Ty said.

"Pictures, huh?" Anisa questioned.

"I have to get going. I'll see you later." Ty ended the call, knowing that he had crossed the line of no return. Now he was all in with no turning back…

"Carlos Delivers A Message."

Bogota, Colombia
September 7, 2013
1:06 p.m.

Carlos was the leader of the Cuadras Cartel operating throughout Mexico and the United States. A once in a lifetime opportunity was on his radar and ready to be had. Mona Moore was incarcerated and her future was unclear, leaving a path for Carlos to strike. It was well known that Carlos and Mona were sworn enemies destined to destroy each other.

Carlos walked into Soria Sanchez's foyer and awaited her arrival. Soria ran Colombia's largest drug ring. Her father, Sergio Sanchez, once ran the family business but was now a political leader in Colombia. He never wanted a life of crime for his only child. It chose her as if she had been preordained. Sergio offered his support by shielding her from the government and hiding her assets. But her business had grown larger than expected, making it more difficult to avoid public scrutiny.

Many years ago, Carlos and his brother Hector, had a business relationship with Sergio Sanchez until he decided to enter politics. This occurred at a time when Hector and Soria had a daughter named Marcella Sanchez. The couple went their separate ways and now Marcella was a young woman working in New York. While Hector had not seen Soria in several years, he felt a certain way about her that was unclear.

Soria was 45 with a youthful appearance. Her sandy-brown hair was long, complimented by her honey-brown eyes, high cheekbones, and soft facial features. Her well-toned body gave her a striking appearance.

"Tell me how long has it been?" Carlos asked as he followed Soria to her office.

"It's been 15 years, but I'm quite sure your absence from my life isn't the reason that brought you to Colombia."

"You're a direct woman and I respect that," Carlos said. "Can old friends have a genuine concern for one another?"

"I don't have any friends in this business," Soria answered.

"Wise woman you are. Well in that case, I came to see your father. Since he made himself unavailable, I'm knocking on your door," Carlos said.

"Whatever business you have with my father, you have with him. I'm in no position to speak or make decisions on his behalf. And I'm not a fan of politics," Soria replied.

"Neither am I," Carlos said.

"Let's cut to the chase as to why you're here," Soria said.

"From my understanding," Carlos said, "you have arrangements with the Sheridan Syndicate and there is no secret of our dealings with Mona. We're not so amicable."

"Carlos, you're contention doesn't present a problem for my operations," Soria said. "Mixing my personal feelings with business isn't a thing I get caught up in."

This conversation was not progressing as Carlos had planned. "Understand that supplying my rival equates to endorsing a war against the Cuadras," Carlos said.

Soria chuckled in disbelief of his audacity to play with her intelligence. "You're a funny guy," Soria said as she folded her arms and grew quiet. Soria's organization was built on a solid foundation and if war was to come, it wouldn't hinder a thing. She was smart and would never allow anyone to push her around. Colombia was her country.

"Are you familiar with the gun manufacturing company, Smith and Wesson?" Soria asked. "They're a global enterprise and have a conduct practiced around the world. Do you think an American emissary considers it treason that they provide guns to their enemies? No! Because it's business and it has nothing to do with the personal feelings of who may not like a particular entity."

"Let's not make light of this situation," Carlos responded. "Whether it's deemed treason or not is immaterial. There are still rules that govern the politics of both worlds. If Smith and Wesson are told to stop selling guns to their enemy, they will comply. It can be arranged for them to be put out of business. So some rules in business can be compromised."

"The only adversary in business is an entity that wants to control it. Dynasties and empires are a common desire in capital. But dynasties fall to greed and empires to internal corruption. They forge war against themselves by their very existence. The only ties that I'm connected to are banks and capital securities. I'm a strong emissary of commerce and capital," Soria explained in no uncertain terms.

"You're a true reflection of your father; just a bit unprincipled in terms of loyalty," Carlos snapped. "I guess the lines have been drawn." Carlos walked to the edge of the balcony and saw two lionesses below. "Why isn't there a male?" Carlos asked with sarcasm.

"Because a male isn't needed," Soria answered. "She hunts her own food and sustains a pride without a weakness."

"Domesticating them must be a challenge. What happens when they feel the need to be what they were designed to be?" Carlos asked.

"You put them down and buy more." Soria understood the hidden message in his line of questioning.

"How's my niece doing these days?" Carlos asked. "Haven't seen her in ages."

"If you try to make any trouble for me or my family, you will regret it. Killing you would not be taken off of the table," Soria threatened. Soria's top lieutenant walked into the room and stood by her. Jesus was her friend and loyalist to her organization. He would kill for her if she so desired.

"You have a good day doll," Carlos said. "Good seeing you. You look great." Carlos left with a hidden agenda.

"If he so much as steps a foot into this country again, you cut his fucking head off and feed it to the lions," Soria said to Jesus as she watched Carlos board his car and drive off.

Sometimes nobody wins, but everybody loses...

Books can be purchased through retail stores, online at Amazon.com, other internet markets, or direct at the following address.

____

Name (Please Print)

____

Address

____

City/State/Zip

***

$20.00 per book includes shipping and handling.

Urban Street Lit
History Publishing Company
% Larry L. Franklin, Editor in Chief
P.O. Box 21
Makanda, Il 62958

CPSIA information can be obtained
at www.ICGtesting.com
Printed in the USA
FFHW020835141219
56865290-62532FF

9 781940 773889